S0-BRQ-752

WITHDRAWN
L. R. COLLEGE LIBRARY

cue met | 21

DR. MARTIN LUTHER

MARTIN OF MANSFELD

BY
MARGARET R. SEEBACH

PHILADELPHIA, PA.
THE UNITED LUTHERAN PUBLICATION HOUSE

Lenoir Rhyne College
LIBRARY

COPYRIGHT, 1916, BY
THE BOARD OF PUBLICATION OF
THE UNITED LUTHERAN CHURCH IN AMERICA

L₁7s
284.1092
Se3m

October, 1939

Biography

16362

TO MY SONS

FOR WHOM I CAN WISH NO BETTER GIFTS
THAN THE COURAGE AND FAITH
OF MARTIN LUTHER

CONTENTS

CONTENTS

ILLUSTRATIONS

PREFACE

MANY years ago, a small girl browsing about in her grandfather's library found a picture of a boy who seemed to be doing just what she was. He had found something that interested him very much in a big book that lay on the floor.

Of course, she wondered what it was; but the words telling her about the picture were long and hard, so she only managed to learn the boy's name, and that of the big book which kept him so busy. She wanted to know more about him. Looking through the book at the other pictures, she found one of him as a man, still busy with the same book. Finally she saw the picture of a great monument, and there the same man stood, still holding the same book.

She thought it too bad that all she could find written about him seemed to be meant for grown-ups. The more she studied the pictures, the more she came to admire and love the man with the book. When she grew old enough to understand some of the big words, she knew that this was one of the world's great heroes, and that the book in his hand represented the secret of all his greatness.

She always thought that it was a pity other boys and girls could not know about him without waiting to grow old enough to read the books that told of him. Now she will tell you, if you listen, the true story of the boy with the big book; for she is sure that if you come to know him, you, too, will love and honor him, and your lives will be better and stronger for having made such a friend as Martin of Mansfeld.

MARGARET R. SEEBACH.

Hollidaysburg, Pa.
June 1, 1916.

ST. MARTIN'S DAY

MARTIN OF MANSFELD

ST. MARTIN'S DAY

"GOOD morning, neighbor Hans? Where are you going so early all in your Sunday clothes?"

It was the eleventh of November, in the year 1483. The late autumn dawn was just brightening over the quiet German town of Eisleben. The old house-mother, who had opened the door of her little home for a breath of the crisp morning air, stood smiling at the young man she had hailed on his early errand; and as he stopped to answer her, his dark face glowed with a proud smile.

"Good morning, and a good day to you and yours, as it is to me and mine!" was his joyous answer. "I go to see the priest about the christening, good neighbor!"

1

"The christening?" exclaimed Mother Liesel, excited at once.

"The christening?" echoed her husband, Gottfried, hobbling to the door as fast as his rheumatism would let him, to look out over his wife's shoulder.

"Last night," said Hans Luther, drawing his short figure to its full height, and feeling at least a head taller than usual, "last night * God sent us a little son—our first-born! And to-day he is to be christened in St. Peter's church, if the priest is willing."

"A boy?" "A little son?" cried the friendly old couple. "The blessing of the saints be upon him!" added pious Liesel. "What will he be named?"

"This is the day of St. Martin," said Hans. "No doubt he will be named for the holy saint. Would Martin Luther not sound well, think you?"

"Aye, aye! and what will you make of him?" inquired old Gottfried with a chuckle. "I wager, as you came along so fast, it was

* Luther was born November 10, 1483.

2

his future you were planning! Will he be a miner, like his father?"

"I cannot say, Father Gottfried," replied the young man, "that I did not plan many things in my mind. If it is in my power and he proves a good scholar, I should like to give him a better chance than I have had. I was thinking I might make him a lawyer, or——"

"Or a professor in the university," laughed the old man, "or a priest, or a bishop, or maybe pope—who knows? A wonderful child, friend Hans! there is nothing he may not become."

Hans Luther laughed and shook his head, starting again on his way. The old couple stood still in the doorway, looking after him with kindly eyes.

"A good, steady man," said Gottfried, approvingly.

"They are good neighbors," said Liesel. "I feel that I have known them long, even though they have lived here only a little

3

while. I must go and see Gretchen * and congratulate her on her boy's coming. She will be a proud mother!"

"I wish," said Gottfried, thoughtfully, "that I had asked him if he needed a loan. It is but lately that they moved here, and now comes the expense of the little one; and the priest, to be sure, will want money for the christening. It makes it hard!"

"Hard, indeed!" said Liesel, turning back into the little house to set upon the table the breakfast of black bread and oatmeal porridge, which latter was steaming in a kettle over the open fire. "Already the priest gets his tenth of all we have—grain, grass, wood, lambs, geese, and chickens! A tenth of all the cheese is his, and the butter and milk; even every tenth egg that my poor hens lay must the father take. Never fear but Hans will pay well for the christening of his little Martin! But he will not begrudge it—so proud is he of his

* Diminutive of Margaret, and used in this book as showing interest and affection.

4

little son. He does not think what it will cost to make him a lawyer!"

But, while old Liesel grumbled over her breakfast porridge, the three bells of St. Peter's church were sounding gaily for the saint's day just begun; and Hans Luther was hastening home again, with a light heart, through the clear November sunshine; and Margaret, his wife, was crooning softly over her tiny boy the old-time lullaby:

"Now sleep, now sleep, my little child;
  He loves thee, Jesus, meek and mild;
  Sweet dreams he'll send, and happy fate;
  He'll make thee wise, and good, and great.
    O Jesus, Master mild,
    Protect my little child!"

5

THE SCHOOLMASTER'S DUNCE

I

THE SCHOOLMASTER'S DUNCE

ALONG an unpaved street of the mining town of Mansfeld, a schoolboy was loitering his way homeward, late in the afternoon. The rugged cliffs, dark with thick woods and pierced by the black shafts of the copper mines, threw their long shadows across the clustering roofs of the little town, which, like Eisleben, a few miles away, lay in the county of Mansfeld.

Six months after little Martin was born, Hans and Margaret Luther with their little boy had come to the town of Mansfeld to live. They were beginning to learn, as the friendly Gottfried and Liesel had predicted, that they must earn more money if their boy was ever to have an education, and

9

here in Mansfeld Hans believed he had a better chance than in Eisleben.

The schoolboy on his homeward way did not whistle or leap; indeed, he walked wearily, and his face was clouded. Once he glanced up at the dark hill where the castle of the counts of Mansfeld frowned over the town; and as he looked he saw the figure of a woman bent beneath a load of broken branches, coming slowly along the road that led from the forest.

"It is my mother," said the boy to himself. "She has been gathering wood for the fire."

He stopped for a moment, as though he would wait for her; then, feeling tenderly of a badly bruised shoulder, he walked on again, shaking his head, having evidently decided that a burden was not the thing for his back at present.

Another turning brought him face to face with several men in grimy clothing, returning from their day's work in the mines. One of them called to him and he waited, knowing his father's voice.

10

"How is it with the school, my son?" asked Hans Luther, as Martin fell into step beside him. "Are you learning well?"

The boy twisted his sore shoulders uneasily and gave his answer in a low tone.

"I do not know, father," he said. "The schoolmaster says we are all dunces and will never learn the Latin."

"But you, Martin, you can rattle off the Latin words fast enough," said Hans, anxiously. "He has had time to make a scholar out of you, surely! Why, when you were so little that you could not climb the hill to the schoolhouse, did not our neighbor's boy, Hans Emler, carry you up on his back? What a little mite you were!"

And, with a hearty laugh, the father struck his boy a sounding blow on the shoulder. Martin winced with pain and great tears started from his eyes.

"How now?" cried Hans, noticing how the boy started and shrank. "Are you so tender that a hand cannot be laid upon you? What ails you, boy?"

11

"My—my shoulder is sore," muttered the boy, unwillingly.

"Ha! has the master been beating you?" exclaimed the father, with sudden suspicion.

"Yes," admitted Martin, very low.

"To-day?"

"Yes, father."

"More than once?"

Martin hesitated so long that his father became vexed, and cried out, sternly,

"Answer me, boy! how often did he whip you to-day?"

"Fifteen times!" cried Martin, in desperation. "But father, I could not help it! He asked me things we had never learned, and beat me when I answered incorrectly. You will not whip me again?"

By this time they were at the door of the little house where the Luthers made their home. Several younger children had been playing on the door-step; but just then they caught sight of the mother approach-

12

ing with her load of firewood, and started on a race to meet her.

Hans drew Martin into the house, and gently commanded him to open his coat. When he saw the bruised shoulders, the father stood so long in silence that the boy looked around fearfully expecting to see a frowning brow. But Hans only turned away, bidding him gruffly to fasten his clothing again, which was finished just as the other children came trooping back to the door.

"Did you see the kobolds in the forest, mother?" questioned one.

"Tell us a story of the gnomes that live in the ground!" cried another, helping to pile the sticks in the corner.

But the mother's quick eye had seen Martin fumbling at his coat-collar, and she put the little ones aside, and went to her eldest son with a look that questioned his act. The bright, dark eyes of the boy, so like her own, met hers frankly, and straightening her weary back, she said

13

cheerily, "If the world smiles not on you and me, the fault is ours, Martin!"

And with this saying, which was a great favorite of hers, Margaret Luther hastened to kindle her fire and prepare the evening meal for her hungry family.

After the simple supper had disappeared and the children had all gone to their early slumbers, Hans and Margaret sat beside the dying embers on the hearth and talked long and earnestly about their plans and wishes for Martin.

"If it had been for a lie or a theft," said the mother, indignantly, "I would not think the master did wrong. Children must suffer for these things or they grow up wicked. I have with my own hand whipped Martin even till the blood came for stealing a single nut. But for not knowing the strange words of the Latin——!"

"It is not so much the beatings," said Hans—for those were the stern days, when parents believed that the rod was not to be spared. "All boys are whipped in school.

14

Hans Luther   MARTIN LUTHER'S PARENTS   Margaret Luther

But it does not seem to me that this man knows how to teach. I mean that Martin shall have as good schooling as I can give him. If only I could afford to send him to Magdeburg! The Null brothers have a good school there. They are not monks, but a teaching brotherhood who are banded together to educate boys, and who teach all good things by preaching and example. Peter Reinicke has a son there."

"Yes, Reinicke!" said Margaret. "He is overseer of the mines, and can well afford to send his son away to school. But how is it with us? All these mouths to feed, and the boy cannot even help! He has no skill at mining; but he must go to school, and even that is not good enough for him—he must be sent away to school, to study with rich men's sons! Not but what the boy is as bright as any of them," she added, with a touch of pride.

"Well, well, Gretchen," said her husband, "I can almost see my way clear to leasing a furnace. If I can do that, I will

15

begin the smelting of the ore instead of mining, and it will pay much better. Then Martin shall go to Magdeburg!''

And rising, with a yawn, he closed the door for the night.

THE SINGER IN THE STREET

II

THE SINGER IN THE STREET

A LITTLE company of schoolboys had just set out across snowy fields from the city of Magdeburg toward an outlying village. The center of interest in the group seemed to be a lad of about fourteen, whose sparkling eyes shone above cheeks that were rather pale and wasted, and whose clear voice rang out through the frosty air, as he declared,

"No, I am quite well again, and the walk will do me good!"

Hans Luther had at last attained his purpose of sending Martin to the school of the Null brothers at Magdeburg. The proceeds of the smelting furnace yielded enough to pay for the schooling and books, but did not provide board and lodging;

and Martin, like other poor scholars, had to earn these by singing from door to door and receiving food in return from the people of the city and neighboring villages.

"We heard that your sickness was very bad, Martin," said one of the lads as they trudged toward the village.

"I thought I was about to die," said Martin, seriously. "I had a burning fever, and, as you know, the doctors say that in such a case one must not drink water."

"Yes, I know it only too well!" said another. "I thought my tongue would wither in my mouth when I was sick a year ago!"

"Well," said Martin, laughing, "it was my good fortune that on Friday, which was a holy day, the people of the house where I stay were all gone to church. I was so wretched that I made up my mind I would have one good, cold drink, if I died of it.

"I was too weak to walk, but I set out to crawl on my hands and knees to the kitchen. It seemed like twenty leagues; but at last I reached it, and there stood a
20

great jug; and oh, thanks to St. Martin, it was full of fresh, cold water!

"So I drank and drank, and when I could drink no more, I crawled back to my bed and fell asleep. When I woke, the fever was gone, and in a few days I was quite strong again."

"St. Martin was kind to you, or else the doctors are all wrong," laughed his friend.

"And now," continued Martin, "since I am getting well, I am as hungry as a wolf, and I could hardly wait to get out and sing again, and earn more food. I was determined to come with you this Christmas eve, for then people may give us cakes instead of bread, and other good things besides."

"Hark to the glutton!" cried another. "But we all like Christmas, for indeed it is a time of plenty, and the poor scholars get their share."

"Besides," added Martin, in a different tone, "there are no songs so beautiful as the Christmas hymns." And he began to hum,

21

in a sweet boyish soprano, the old German carol,

"A little babe, so pure and blest."

"Yes, that is very well for you," said one boy, in a complaining tone. "You have a good voice and love to sing! As for me, I grow sick of trailing from door to door singing songs that mean nothing to me, and getting a crust now and then like a beggar! If I did not look forward to a day when I shall be learned and rich and do as I please, I could not endure it!"

"Men do harder things than that," said Martin Luther, his dark eyes growing soft and deep with the vision. "I can never forget what I saw since I came to Magdeburg. You know what I mean—the Prince of Anhalt, who has laid aside his title and rank and entered the monastery; how he goes in the coarse garb of a monk, so thin from fasting that he can hardly stagger up and down the streets with a sack on his back, begging bread for the brothers in

22

the convent! Our trials are nothing to his!

"And often, in my home in Mansfeld," he continued, "I have seen the pilgrims going to the holy places in the neighborhood, coming from miles around to have their diseases taken away; and those too weak to walk were carried to some place where they could hear the bells of Wimmelberg church, believing that the very sound would make them well.

"And I saw the child-pilgrims—little boys and girls, eleven hundred from Eisleben alone—following the standard of the red cross to Wilsnach without money or food, begging their way as they journeyed. Some were not eight years old, but it was said that in a day and a night, they marched eighty miles! They were ready to drop, yet——"

"Here we are!" whispered another. "This is a large, fine farmhouse; let us sing here first."

The little group gathered close about the door, and presently the notes of a carol

23

rang out, with the clear, sweet voice of Martin leading:

"In sweetest exultation
Let every voice arise;
Our Hope and Consolation
Within a manger lies!"

Suddenly a harsh voice broke in upon the melody. The door of the house was flung open, and the farmer appeared, crying roughly:

"Where are you, young rascals?"

Terrified by such a reception, the boys broke and fled, their scanty scholars' gowns flapping about their heels as they ran. They expected no less than a beating if the farmer caught them; and still the loud voice kept roaring after them, increasing their fright.

But Martin caught a note of laughter in the harsh shouts, and rallied the timid singers.

"Look, look! it is not a club he has in his hands; he is holding two great, big sausages, and calling us to come and get them."

24

Fearful still, but resolved to have the sausages, the boys at last came back and received the gift amid roars of laughter from the burly farmer. They thanked him heartily, finished their interrupted song, and trudged on to the clustered lights of the village.

"Mother, do listen!" exclaimed the little daughter of Conrad Cotta, a wealthy citizen of Eisenach. "The boys are singing at the door; and what a beautiful voice one of them has!"

Ursula Cotta came and stood at the window beside her little girl. A fair, stately woman she was, smiling beneath the snowy cap of the German house-mother, with her long, white apron embroidered across the bottom, her velvet pouch and bunch of keys dangling at her side, and her look of quiet, matronly dignity.

"He has a fine face," she said, half to herself. "A good face. Poor boy, how thin he looks!"

25

And, stepping to the door, she called the singers to enter.

Martin Luther, whose sweet voice had won the attention of the good Ursula, had spent only a year in Magdeburg. Then Hans had remembered that he had a number of relatives living in Eisenach, and decided to send Martin to the school in that place.

But the relatives were not wealthy people, and Martin's poverty was little bettered by the change of abode. He still went about the streets singing for his daily bread, and now and then receiving a little money.

The house of the Cottas was warm and cozy, compared with the poor lodgings where Martin spent most of his nights. We should not think it very comfortable, with its bare walls and carpetless floors, and only the great fireplace giving out a fitful heat; but nobles and princes had few better houses in those days, and this was a home of luxury, contrasted with many in Eisenach.

26

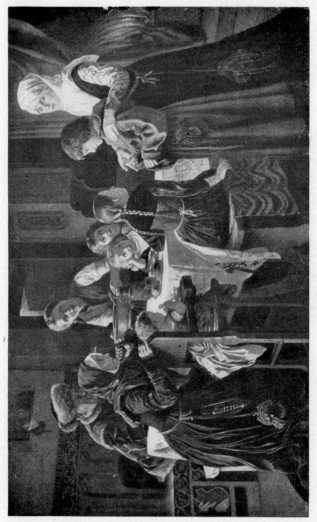

"THE HOME OF THE COTTAS WAS WARM AND COZY"

There was good soup and plenty of bread for the singers. Dame Ursula cut it with her own plump hands and waited on them like a mother, asking meantime kindly questions about their homes and parents. The little folks came up shyly and watched the singers while they ate, and afterward begged for more songs.

As the boys were leaving, Dame Ursula held Martin back a moment.

"I want you to visit us often again," she said softly. "Come back after your school hours; I want to talk with you and hear you sing."

The children clapped their hands at the words.

From that day Martin felt that he had a new home. Much of his time was spent with the Cottas, and his hollow cheeks began to fill out under the influence of the good things he shared at Dame Ursula's table. Cold and hunger were things of the past, and a happy home circle gladdened his lonely heart.

27

So passed four happy years. And no less improved was Martin's treatment in school.

"Our master, the learned Trebonius," he told Dame Ursula, "never comes into the schoolroom in the morning without taking off his cap to us. One of the boys asked him why he did it, and he said: 'I take off my cap before the future mayor, chancellor, or learned doctor whom God may have chosen any of you, my pupils, to become.'"

"And so they may, Martin," said his motherly friend. "You yourself may be called to a great work, and you must be ready for it."

"The saints grant it!" said Martin devoutly.

At length came word from Mansfeld. Hans Luther was prospering, and had now two furnaces instead of one. Martin was to leave Eisenach, and enter the university at Erfurt, there to realize his father's fondest hopes by studying to prepare himself for the profession of law.

28

A PROUD FATHER

A PROSPEROUS PLACE

THE household of Hans Luther was all
neat, and cheerful estate in such that
some great deal of land, such comforts—
thing and plenty and nothing ... and hard-
ing. And, indeed, there was plenty to do,
for the home was no home; the little house
to which Hans used to come home with the
toil of the ... upon him, and from which
his good Gretchen went out to gather the
fagots for the fire.

Hans had prospered, and was now a
citizen of note in Mansfield. He had built
a house befitting his position, and the family
was now preparing to receive ... that child
the son of whom his parents were, indeed,
proud.

Four years ago, a group of settlers had

III

A PROUD FATHER

THE household of Hans Luther was all astir, and it could easily be seen that some great event was at hand. Such scrubbing and polishing, such baking and brewing! And, indeed, there was plenty to do; for the home was no longer the little house to which Hans used to come home with the soil of the mines upon him, and from which his good Gretchen went out to gather the fagots for the fire.

Hans had prospered, and was now a citizen of note in Mansfeld. He had taken a house befitting his means; and the family was now preparing to receive a visit from the son of whom his parents were justly proud.

Four years ago, a youth of seventeen had

enrolled at the University of Erfurt as "Martin Luther, from Mansfeld." To-day he was coming home in triumph, having lately received his degree as Master of Arts, standing second in his class.

"Here he comes! Oh, father, mother, here is Martin!" screamed the younger children, and all the neighborhood flocked out to see their scholar. While his horse was being led away to the stable, he held quite a reception, greeting heartily the well-known faces, seen but seldom during those years of absence.

"Will you not come within?" queried Hans, holding open the door for his son with deep respect. Martin looked at him in surprise; for his father had never spoken to him in that tone before.

"Come in, I pray you!" repeated Hans Luther; and Martin saw that his father's eyes were full of the tears of happy pride.

All day Hans and Margaret waited on their Master of Arts with every mark of honor, until his modest soul could endure it no longer.

"Ah, my father!" at length he exclaimed, when the visitors were gone, and parents and son were alone at last. "Be not so ceremonious with your boy! What am I but your Martin, even as before?"

"You are now a scholar, my son," replied Hans, seriously, "and I do honor to Master Martin Luther!"

"Have you never heard the saying," laughed Martin, "that in Erfurt there are as many Masters of Art as there are stones in the pavement?" Then, seeing his father's look of disappointment, he added quickly, "But indeed it is a glorious thing to attain to one's degree! When our examinations were passed, we were taken in procession through the streets by our fellow students, with banners, torches, and music, and all the people of Erfurt saluting us as 'Master' on this side and on that. What a moment of majesty and splendor was that! It seems to me that no earthly joy can equal it."

"Tell us about your days at Erfurt, my son," begged Margaret, sitting close beside her boy. "You have been away so long, and we have known so little of what you were doing! Tell me not of your strange studies with the names I cannot set my mouth to pronounce; tell me rather of your companions, and how your time was spent outside of your schoolrooms."

"There was one," said Martin, thoughtfully, "who was there when I entered, but three years ahead of me. His name was George Spalatin, and I learned to know him very well. He is a man I would fain keep all my life for a friend. There was another, Lange by name, whom also I think I shall never forget. There was young Eoban Hess, who entered but a year ago; a brilliant lad, a poet and scholar such as seldom comes even to Erfurt.

"There was a man of another sort," he went on, breaking into a laugh, "who was my room-mate for a couple of years. How he hated study! I do not think he ever took up a book unless I lectured him soundly for his indolence. One day, when I had been scolding him, he sat down with a book in his hand, and after glaring at it angrily for half an hour he suddenly threw it on the floor and stamped on it, exclaiming: 'You want to make a fool of me, do you? From the word "study" comes the word "stupid." Study always makes dunces!' And he tramped off, leaving the book on the floor for me to pick up! It was not all study, though; we had happy times of good fellowship with jesting and song.

"Once I hurt my leg and was laid up for some time by the accident. I had not been long in the rooms where I then was, the people were strange to me, and, though they were kind, I was very lonely and the hours hung heavy on my hands.

"At last, rummaging about in a large closet in the wall, I found an old lute. How rejoiced I was! It was out of repair, but

I strung it up and thrummed on it all day long! I taught myself to play a little, though I had no teacher, and when I was well again, I took it to some of our merry gatherings, and the students were delighted to have a little accompaniment to their songs. They called me 'the musician' after that!"

"You never forgot your prayers, Martin?" asked the mother wistfully. His face lit up with a new brightness as he answered:

"My motto, through all my school-days, has been, 'To pray well is to study well.' Every day I began with prayer, dear mother.

"I found something one day that was wonderful to me, and I wish I had it for my own. I was looking for a book in the library at the university, when I found a book I had never seen before. It was the Word of God, in Latin; the whole of it, not just the parts we hear in church; and I opened it to see what it was like.

"Mother, it opened at the story of Han-

36

"I FOUND SOMETHING ONE DAY THAT WAS WONDERFUL. . . . IT WAS
THE WORD OF GOD IN LATIN"

nah, the mother of Samuel; how she prayed to God to give her a son, and she would devote him to the service of God; and when he was old enough, she took him to God's house and left him there with the old priest. And one night the Lord spoke to him in a vision. But then it was time to go to my next lecture, and I could read no more.

"But it made me think of my own good mother, and wonder if the Lord would ever call me to carry a message for him. And if he does," said Martin, with deep reverence, "I want to be ready to answer him, and say, 'Speak, for thy servant heareth,' just as Samuel did."

And Father Hans, from his corner by the hearth, uttered a long sigh, and had no word to say; but pious Mother Margaret, holding her boy's hand in her work-hardened fingers, said clearly and tenderly, "Amen!"

A DAY OF DECISION

IV

A DAY OF DECISION

IT was now time for Martin to take up the actual study of law, if he were going to fulfil his father's ambition. Hans would hear of no delay. Regardless of expense he purchased for his son the costly books he would require, and sent him back to Erfurt in time for the opening of the law school in May.

Martin was not enthusiastic about the study of law.

"Lawyers," he once remarked, "say a great deal and use many words, but without understanding. They take the money of the poor, and with their tongue thresh out both their pocket and their purse."

But his father wished him to become a lawyer, and he entered upon the task obediently, if not joyfully.

The spring and summer of 1505 were times of trouble at Erfurt. The terrible disease known as the plague broke out, and the students as well as the townspeople were attacked by it. Some died of it, others fled from the city in a panic. One of Martin's particular friends among the students died about this time, and a great sadness filled the mind of the young scholar.

Besides, the law studies became more distasteful to him every day. More and more his mind turned toward the thought of God who called Samuel, and who might even now be calling him to a different sort of work.

"I am not making the most of my life," he often said to himself. "I am given up to worldly studies and pursuits instead of being devoted to something that would help to save my own soul and the souls of others."

Again and again there came to him the memory of the pilgrims he had seen thronging to the holy shrines; of the Prince of

Anhalt carrying his sack of broken bits, begging for food on the streets of Magdeburg; of the monks of a little monastery near Eisenach with whom he had been very friendly while he lived with the Cotta family.

"Surely," he thought, "the best way of pleasing God is to do as these have done; to deny oneself all ease and pleasure, to withdraw from the world, and to give one's whole life to prayers and deeds of charity!"

There came back to him now the remembrance of a painting he had seen in a church while he was at school at Magdeburg.

"It was a great ship," he reminded himself, "sailing safely on stormy waters. On its deck was the pope, with his cardinals and bishops around him. All the crew were priests and monks. The ship was the Church, and it was bound for the harbor of heaven.

"All about, in the water, were the poor people who were neither monks nor priests but just common men like myself. Here

43

and there one of the crew flung out a rope from the vessel for one of them to grasp; but most of them were sinking in the waves. Only those on board were safe!"

So heavily did these thoughts weigh upon him that about the last of June he went home to Mansfeld for a short visit, hoping to talk the matter over with his father and get permission at least to give up the study of law.

"Do not venture to speak to your father of such a thing!" counseled his mother, to whom he hinted his intention. "All his pride and his hope are in you, and it will break his heart to have you give up your studies. Already he plans a good marriage for you which will connect us with a wealthy family. Anger him not; go back, my son, and pray to the good God to make your way clear!"

Martin stayed but a few days at home. He was so thoroughly out of harmony with his father's joyous predictions of a brilliant

44

career that on the second of July he left Mansfeld to return to Erfurt.

The air was close and oppressive, but he chose to walk rather than to ride, hoping that the exercise would help to throw off the gloomy thoughts that filled his mind. He felt like a prisoner whom love and duty held faster than iron bars.

"I am a coward!" he told himself. "I know that I am doing wrong, yet I am too weak to tell my father! Truly his disappointment would be great. But if my father's anger would be terrible, how much more dreadful would be the wrath of God! He might justly punish me for my disobedience."

The sky darkened more and more as he went on, but he scarcely noticed it. All through the sultry afternoon he tramped the dusty roads, his dark eyes clouded with trouble.

The evening was drawing near and he was close to the little village of Stotternheim,

45

only a few miles outside of Erfurt, when the gathering storm broke in fury.

It was too late to seek shelter. The wind swept vast waves of dust up from the road, stifling and blinding him; the darkness grew more and more dense; the lightnings cleft the gloom like the sword of an angry angel, and the thunder seemed to shake the very foundations of the earth.

Martin struggled on, scarcely knowing in what direction he went. All the wrong acts he had ever done, all his doubts about the future, all his fears of the God who now appeared to him as an awful Judge rather than as the Friend who spoke to Samuel—all these thoughts seemed to have taken the form of dreadful demons, and to be pursuing him.

Suddenly a blaze of blue flame split the darkness close beside him. A dazzling ball of fire aimed, as it seemed, directly at his head came plunging through the tempest, to disappear in the ground only a few feet from where he stood. A clap of thunder

46

followed which rattled like a roll of musketry about him.

Martin fell half dazed upon the ground. For a few moments the violence of the shock held him unable to move or think. Still the storm raged and beat upon him. Presently struggling to his knees he clasped his hands and tried to pray. The wind snatched the words from his mouth, and carried them away with mocking shrieks. Desperate with fear in the midst of the tumult, words sprang to his lips as though some power stronger than himself had forced them from him.

"Help me, dear St. Anna!" he gasped. "Save me, and I will become a monk!"

Then he fell exhausted and lay trembling on the rain-beaten earth.

The storm had almost spent its force. In a few minutes the wind began to subside; the lightning flashes grew more remote, and the thunder rumbled farther and farther away.

At last, as Martin lay on the ground, he

ventured to open his eyes and saw that it was growing lighter. He rose again to his knees, and, behold! a shaft of golden light from the setting sun shone full into his lifted face. He stretched his hands to meet it, and felt that St. Anna had accepted his vow.

It was a drenched and silent student who reached his lodgings late that evening. During the next few days his friends wondered greatly what had happened to Martin. His merry laugh was hushed, his lute was hidden, and he went about like a man in a dream.

About two weeks after the storm they learned the meaning of the change. The students to whom he was most attached, and a few of the townspeople in whose homes he had been intimate, received little notes of invitation, which caused them further surprise.

"Come and take supper with me on the sixteenth," wrote Martin. "I have a heavy

48

"SLOWLY THE HEAVY DOOR SWUNG OPEN; AND WHEN IT CLOSED IT
HID THE BELOVED FORM OF THEIR 'MUSICIAN'"

task before me, and would first spend a pleasant evening with my friends."

When the little company was gathered, it seemed as though they must have misread the mysterious words of the note. Never had Martin seemed happier. His voice and lute led them, after supper was over, in song after song. All the lively pranks and jests of student life, all the happy times he had spent in Erfurt he recounted with relish.

"Martin is himself again to-night," whispered his friends to one another, delighted to see him so cheerful. "It is long since he has shown so merry a face."

At length the lute was laid aside, and Martin rose and stood looking about upon his guests.

"Dear friends," he said—and there was no merriment now upon his lips—"I have called you together to say farewell. Once more I have enjoyed your good company, but it is the last time. To-morrow I shall enter the monastery here in Erfurt to save

49

your souls and mine by penances and prayers, if God and the holy saints be gracious."

A clamor of remonstrance arose. There were tears and protestations, but all in vain. Nothing could change his purpose or alter the firm lines of his quiet lips.

The next morning, a few of the students walked sorrowfully with him to the gate of the monastery, and waited while he knocked for admission.

Slowly the heavy door swung open; and when it closed, it hid the beloved form of their "musician" from their tearful eyes.

THE FIRST MASS

V

"GOOD morning, neighbor Gretchen. I have come to see how you are, now that the excitement is over, and the men are off at last on their way to Erfurt."

The comely face of Anna Klein, neighbor and friend of the Luthers, wore a broad smile, which was quickly reflected on the lips of Margaret Luther.

"Good morning, Anna. Yes, indeed, there was excitement this morning while they were getting ready to go. Never in his life was my Hans so particular about the putting on of his best suit, and the polishing of the buckles on his horse's harness. 'We must not shame him,' he kept saying. 'We must do honor to Martin, and to Mansfeld, too!'"

"They will make a fine showing, truly," said Anna. "Twenty riders, all in their best, bringing liberal gifts for the monastery!"

"There will be some from Eisenach, too," said Margaret. "Martin wrote that he had invited my kinsman, Conrad Hutter, who lives there, and the priest, Father Braun, who is a good friend of his."

"It is a great occasion, when the young priest holds his first mass," said Anna. "It would have been a pleasant thing for you to go along, Gretchen."

"What should I do among all the men?" laughed Margaret. "They will talk of great matters that a plain, unlearned woman cannot understand; and I would be left sitting in a corner! I was glad enough to see Hans go," she added, more gravely.

"It is almost two years since he has seen Martin, is it not?" asked Anna. Her friend nodded.

"Not since he entered the monastery,"

54

she said. "Indeed, I thought he would never consent to see him again."

"He was terribly angry when the news came that Martin was going to be a monk," said Anna. "I remember how my husband and other friends came and tried to reason with him, but he would hear nothing."

"Never since I have known him," said Margaret Luther, "was Hans so enraged; I dared not say a word to him. I take blame to myself, too; for I knew that Martin wanted to give up his studies, and I would not let him tell his father. That was what angered him most—that Martin never told him. But he is a good son and a loving one, and would not have disappointed his father except that he believed God called him."

"Hans has softened much in the last year," remarked Anna.

"Yes, since our two younger boys died of the plague, and the report came to us that Martin was also dead," said the mother, with a sigh. "Hans is still grieved that Martin is a monk, yet he is proud of him, too. He was always so proud of Martin!"

"He will be prouder of him yet," prophesied Anna, drawing her cloak about her. "Martin is no ordinary young man. Well, good-by, Gretchen. I must go and bake some bread; Peter took along all I had for a lunch upon the way."

The service was over.

Hans Luther came out of the church a little behind his Mansfeld friends, drawing his rough old hand hastily across his eyes.

He was trying to realize that the earnest young priest whom he had just seen performing the most sacred ceremony of the Church—the mass, or communion service— was really his own son, Martin.

It was not the priestly robes that made him look different; nor the hollowness of his pale cheeks; nor even the head shaven about the crown—the badge of the monk.

It was the look on his face that changed

56

him so; the look of deep reverence, almost fear; of humility and self-distrust, and yet of something lofty; the look that made Hans know, for the first time, how much the new-made priest took to heart his profession.

"If he must be a priest," the father said to himself, "he will be a good one. He does not take it lightly, as so many do. How he trembled as he read the mass! Once he stopped as if he were overcome, and looked around almost as if he would run away. My heart stood still for fear he would break down.

"He does not look, either, like one of the fat, selfish, monks who live idly in the monasteries, gorging themselves on what they squeeze out of the poor people. He has been fasting, not feasting!

"He means well, and he will try to do what is right; but things will never be as we had hoped!

"Well, to-night comes the banquet; then we shall feel more at home!"

But when he was seated that evening at the banquet, in the place of honor beside his son, Hans was not more at ease. Not only the good neighbors from Mansfeld were there, but Martin's more distinguished and scholarly friends of Erfurt; for this was one occasion when they might all meet and rejoice with him.

As the conversation became more and more animated, the brilliance of Martin's share in it marked him out as the master of them all. No humor was so sparkling as his, no replies so ready; and on more serious themes he was equally at home. Hans found himself thinking with regret of the magnificent lawyer Martin would have made!

At last, before he knew it, a deep sigh broke from the father's lips. Martin, who was in the midst of a clever retort, stopped instantly, and turned to him.

"What is wrong, dear father?" he asked anxiously. Hans could conceal his feelings no longer.

58

"I must sit here," he exclaimed impatiently, "and eat and drink, when I would much rather be anywhere else!"

"Is it not a time of joy to you, my father?" asked Martin, gently. "Are you not now content, seeing what a holy calling I have entered? Why were you so angry with me, and would not forgive my becoming a monk?"

"Did you never hear," said Hans, lifting his gray head with dignity, "that a son must be obedient to his parents?" Then, turning to the company who were now listening intently, he continued:

"And you, learned men, did you never read in the Scripture, 'Thou shalt honor thy father and thy mother'?"

Silence reigned for a moment. The young priest sat with bowed head.

"But, neighbor Hans," spoke up honest Peter Klein, from Mansfeld, "Martin had a sign from God—a call from heaven. Is not God to be obeyed, above father and mother?"

"God grant it be so!" said Hans Luther, his rugged face working with strong emotion. "I have yet to be convinced that it was not a trick of the Evil One, who loves to deceive!"

With these words he rose from the table.

"Martin," he said, with open arms, "embrace me now and let us say farewell. To-morrow morning, with the dawn, we ride home again to Mansfeld."

BROTHER MARTIN

VI

BROTHER MARTIN

A LITTLE group of monks had gathered in the cloister of the monastery at Erfurt, on a quiet summer evening. The center of attention was a man of middle age, with a stern and care-worn face, who had just come out of the main building.

"I beg of you, my brothers, do not be excited," he was saying. "The report you have heard is untrue. Our brother is not dead, though for a time he lay unconscious. He is now reviving, and I have sent to him his confessor whose presence he desires."

"May we ask, father," inquired one, "why the choristers were sent for?"

"Here they come!" said the subprior. "They can tell you themselves; business of importance calls me elsewhere."

63

"It seems to me," said another, looking after the subprior's retreating figure, "that the reverend father is unusually short in his answers."

"My own dull wits," remarked a third, "would almost lead me to imagine that he is displeased at Brother Martin for not being really dead!"

"It must be a disappointment!" laughed the second. "Think what a great thing for the convent, if we could have taken credit for a new saint!"

"Well, we shall have one, sooner or later, if Martin persists in his penances!" said the other. "But wait!" he cried out to the choristers, who were hastening past. "Tell us why you were summoned to Brother Martin's cell."

Two of the singers shook their heads and hurried on; but the third, a rosy, good-natured little man, came and sat down on a bench near the group, and answered readily:

"Oh, Martin has been fasting and torturing himself again. You know what a persistent fellow he is; the ordinary rules of the convent were not enough for him, and he has made out a set of extra ones for himself. Flesh and blood cannot endure what he inflicts on himself."

"But you are not answering our question, Brother Thomas," said several, impatiently.

"Wait, wait, good brothers!" said the little man, who rather enjoyed his importance of the moment. "I will tell you all about it.

"You know, Brother Martin is exceedingly fond of music. He believes that when the Evil One tempts us, music can drive him away; and truly," he added, with great self-satisfaction, "I cannot say I ever suffer many temptations. It must be because I am always busy about the music!"

"Go on! Go on!" was the chorus.

"Well, to-day the foolish fellow has been shut in his cell since early morning. He has fasted since day before yesterday, has

65

kept vigil all last night upon his knees, and this morning Brother Stephen, whose cell is next to his, heard blows of the lash resounding.''

"What a holy life he leads!" cried one enthusiastic brother.

"Holy—yes, but very uncomfortable!" declared Brother Thomas, rubbing his fat sides, and stretching himself with a yawn. "Of course, he fainted again! Stephen heard him fall, and called the subprior. They had to burst the door open, and it was a long time before he came to himself."

"But what had you to do with it all?" said an eager listener.

"When he first opened his eyes," said Thomas, "he stared so wildly, and muttered so foolishly, that they thought his mind unbalanced. So the subprior sent Brother Stephen for us; and as we chanted our hymns, slowly he grew calm, and at last he looked at us with reason in his eyes.

"Music is great, my brothers, and wonderful is its power; but now I think the best thing to do would be to give him something to eat!"

"You are a worldly-minded man, Thomas!" declared one, laughing. "You have no fancy for becoming a saint! But indeed, no such devotion as Brother Martin's has been known in this house for many years. Should he die, many miracles would be performed here, and much money would flow into our coffers. I am almost sorry for the subprior!"

"Nay, I would not see our Martin die, even to be made a saint," said another monk. "He is a lovable man, and as pious and humble as he is devoted. Do you remember, when first he entered here as a novice, how some of the brothers thought he would be proud, because he was known in all Erfurt as a fine scholar?"

"Yes, and I remember," said Thomas, "how meekly he did all the menial services that were laid upon him—sweeping and scrubbing, and begging from door to door. 'He is no better than we,' some jealous

67

ones said. 'Let the proud scholar take the sack on his shoulder, and go into the streets, to beg of his former friends!' "

"That made no difference to Martin," said the other. "In fact, he was so eager for discipline that he wished for more burdens to be added rather than to have less than others."

"Listen!" said a brother, "I hear the sound of carriage wheels without."

And presently a monk from within the building announced that the vicar-general of their order, Dr. John Staupitz, had come unexpectedly to visit the monastery and would remain a few days.

"I am glad of that!" said Thomas, trotting along more briskly than usual, as they all hastened to greet their honored head. "Brother Martin loves Dr. Staupitz and honors him above all men. Perhaps he can get him to listen to reason."

"Not if the subprior can help it!" remarked his nearest neighbor in a whisper.

It was not until the next morning that

the vicar-general entered the little cell where Martin lay.

"Do not rise, my son!" said the good man, as Martin tried to greet him, and sank back in extreme weakness. "What is this you have been doing to yourself?"

"Oh, my father!" said Martin, extending a wasted hand, "my sufferings are nothing compared with my sins! If I could wipe them out by fasting and scourging, how gladly would I do it!"

"What are your sins, my son?" inquired the great man kindly. "Let me judge whether they are deserving of such severe punishment."

"They are grievous, dear father!" said the young man. "Twice in the past week have I fallen asleep over my prayers; three times have I made mistakes in repeating the words of the mass. Many vain and idle thoughts pursue and tempt me by night and day to forget my duties."

"Brother Martin," said the superior, gravely, "have you no real sins to confess? These are painted sins—a mere picture and no reality. Your very fasting and watching have brought you to a state where such mistakes and omissions are natural. How can you stay awake, when you are dying for sleep? How can you help forgetting, when you are weak unto starvation? Are these all your sins?"

"Alas, no!" sighed Martin. "I am of a proud and hasty temper, and often feel impatient with others. Sometimes I envy those who are peaceful and happy; sometimes I feel rebellious at the demands of God, who by a dreadful experience drove me into the convent."

"Now you are speaking of real sins, my son," said Dr. Staupitz. "What is the cure for these? What did your confessor tell you, when he was with you last night?"

"He reminded me," said Martin, "that we say, in the Apostles' Creed, 'I believe in the forgiveness of sins.'"

"Ah!" said Staupitz, "Have you asked that your sins be forgiven?"

"Yes, yes! but how can I be sure of it?"

"Only by believing in Christ, my son!"

"In Christ!" said Martin, with a shudder. "I am afraid to speak to him! Twenty-one saints have I chosen to be my special patrons; each day I pray to three, so that in a week I have invoked them all. But how shall I speak to the great Lord of all?"

"That is not our dear Lord Christ of whom you are afraid," said Dr. Staupitz. "Christ does not terrify; he only consoles. Leave your prayers to the saints, your fasting and penances, and learn all you can of Christ."

And, rising, he blessed the young monk, laying his hand tenderly on Martin's head.

"He is a youth of a noble spirit," he said to the subprior, whom he met outside the door of the little cell, "but he is carrying his penance too far, and will kill himself if he keeps on. He needs outside interests and work for others. I have a plan in mind which I think will help him."

"What strange advice," mused Martin, in his cell. "The subprior is always saying it is more discipline we need! But Father Staupitz is not like any of the others." And, rising on one elbow, he reached out to the table beside him, where the red leather cover of his Latin Bible made the one spot of brightness in the gloomy cell.

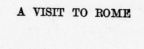

A VISIT TO ROME

VII

A VISIT TO ROME

A FLAT, sandy plain; a walled town wherein dwelt a few thousand people in low, frame houses mostly thatched with straw; and, looking down upon this dreary prospect, two large churches—the Town Church and the Castle Church—and a monastery where a new university was finding its first home; this was Wittenberg.

Martin Luther looked about him with homesick eyes. After the beautiful wooded hills among which he had always lived, this poorly-built town, with the river Elbe winding past its gates, had little attraction for him.

"He has sent me to the very borders of the civilized world," he said to himself, "but I would go anywhere for Dr. Staupitz;

besides, he is my superior and it is my duty to obey.''

This was the change the good Doctor had planned for Brother Martin. The great Elector,* Frederick the Wise, had lately founded a university at Wittenberg; Dr. Staupitz was its dean, and he had summoned Martin to leave the cloisters at Erfurt and come to Wittenberg to teach in the new college.

To his friend, the good Father Braun in Eisenach, Martin wrote soon after:

''Wonder not that I departed without saying farewell. For my departure was so sudden that it was almost unknown to my fellow monks. Now I am at Wittenberg, by God's command or permission, I am well, but my duties are very severe.''

There was no more time for mourning over sins, real or imaginary. Hard but healthful work was Martin's now—teaching

* One of the seven great princes who at that period had the right of electing the emperor.

76

and studying himself that he might teach better.

But a greater event was near at hand. A year or two after going to Wittenberg, while back at Erfurt for a time, the sub-prior called him into his room.

"Brother Martin," he said, "you know that Brother John of Mecheln is going to Rome, on business for Dr. Staupitz. It is not fitting that he should travel alone, and we have chosen you to be his companion."

Martin bowed low in assent.

"This is a great opportunity for you, Brother Martin," continued the subprior. "To tread the ground where the blessed apostles and martyrs dwelt; to pray at the holy shrines and gain merit from the saints; perhaps to see the Holy Father, the Pope— these are wonderful privileges."

Martin expressed his thanks, and left the cell like one in a dream. To see Rome, the Eternal City! the center and capital of the Christian world—this was joy for which he had never dared to hope. Now, surely, he would find peace from his temptations and satisfaction for his soul!

Since Dr. Staupitz had talked with him, he had read much in his Latin Bible and had come to know Christ better; but he still felt that he must have the saints to stand between him and the Son of God, and believed that God was pleased and that man earned merit by prayers and penances.

"I will visit every shrine at Rome," he said to himself, "I will pray at every holy place. If I cannot find holiness at Rome, it is nowhere in the world."

It was a bright October day when Brother John and Brother Martin set out from Erfurt. They were not allowed to walk side by side, spending the time in conversation, but must walk silently, in single file. Brother John was much occupied with the thought of the business on which he was sent; but the bright eyes of Martin were busy along the way, on this his first real journey.

The whole way was taken on foot, so that

78

he had plenty of time to see all that was about him. From monastery to monastery they went, stopping with the brothers for entertainment, and then setting out again.

Across the Alps they journeyed; then down over the fertile plains of Lombardy into Italy the beautiful.

Now it was hard for Martin to keep silence, trudging behind his unheeding companion. Such grapes and peaches, such oranges and lemons, he had never seen! The river Po, flowing between the Alps and the Apennines, struck him with wonder and amazement.

"A merry water!" he murmured to himself, as he journeyed along its banks. "Truly a prince among rivers!"

The mild climate was another surprise; but he and his companion soon found that it was more treacherous, if softer, than the air of their colder land.

"How wretched I feel!" said Martin to Brother John, when they arose one morning. "I have a fever, and pain in my head."

"It is the air!" said John ruefully. "We should have known better than to sleep with open windows in this marshy country. I also have fever, and a raging thirst."

That was a hard day for the travelers. In spite of sickness, they plodded on. At last the thirst became too great.

"Brother John," said Martin, in desperation, "I can endure it no longer! I must drink some of this fair, flowing water!"

"It is deadly!" said John, rousing himself. "Do not touch it! The fever will pass away, but the water is poisonous! Come, Martin, it is not pure, like our mountain streams; do not look at it!"

They toiled on, the hot landscape swimming before their fevered eyes. At last Brother John turned joyfully to the lagging Martin.

"Look! God has sent us fruit to quench our thirst!"

80

And he pointed to a stone wall over which there hung a branch freighted with two luscious pomegranates.

How delicious the sweet juice was to their parched throats! After this they traveled on less painfully, and by evening the fever was gone.

At last, after a journey of some six weeks, they reached the hilltop from which the traveler catches the first glimpse of the city of Rome lying outspread upon its seven hills, with the Tiber winding below.

To Martin the sight was overwhelming.

"Hail, holy Rome!" he cried aloud, falling on his knees, with arms outstretched toward the city.

Brother John crossed himself devoutly, but wasted no time in raptures.

"Come, Brother Martin, we must reach the gates before nightfall. The city is still some miles away, and the whole country around is infested with robbers who may even be greedy enough to rob poor monks like us!"

During the next four weeks Martin hastened from shrine to shrine, visiting every holy place in Rome. To those who did this the Church promised forgiveness of all their sins as well as freedom from the torments of purgatory, through which they were taught that men must pass before entering heaven.

Ten times while in Rome he said mass; but he found this very different from the solemn service in the church at Erfurt.

The Italian priests were careless and irreverent. Many would be saying masses at neighboring altars in the same church at one time.

"These priests," complained Martin to Brother John, "read seven masses while I am finishing one! They hurry through as if it were a jest; and then they cry out at me, 'Hurry, hurry! you are too slow!' They have no reverence for sacred things!"

"Many things in Rome are not as they are with us," said John, gravely.

And so Martin found it to be. There

82

were careless and unworthy priests in all places but at Rome the spirit of irreverence was general. The thirst for money was in the souls of the clergy from the pope down, and Martin was often sick at heart to see how the priests cheated and mocked the people who trusted them.

From these things he turned with relief to the sacred shrines.

"The apostles and saints, at least, are true!" he said to himself. "Here the holy Peter walked! here Paul the aged lay in prison, and went forth at last to his martyrdom! I will pray to them and to all the other saints to be kept from the sins I see about me."

He sought the churches where relics of the saints were displayed for worship—a bone of one, the hair of another, a piece of the true cross—all falsehoods, by means of which the priests got money from the believing people.

Last and greatest of all he sought the

83

Holy Staircase near the church of St. John.

This was a stone stairway, said to have been brought from Jerusalem where it formed part of the palace of Pilate, and was trodden by the feet of the Savior at the time of his trial. These stairs the devout pilgrim was expected to climb on his knees; and for every step he was granted nine years' indulgence, or forgiveness for all sins he might commit.

Up these stairs Martin set out to climb laboriously, pausing at every step to offer prayers.

Suddenly in the middle of the flight of steps he stopped.

Clearly and unmistakably a voice had spoken to him. Not with his ears, but in the depths of his heart he heard it; and the words were those he had read so often in his Latin Bible:

"The just shall live by faith."

Not by doing acts of merit, not by prayers and penances, just by believing in

84

Christ, the pardoner of sins! It was just what Dr. Staupitz had told him long ago at Erfurt.

"What are you doing here, Martin?" he said to himself. "This is not the way to please God!"

If any one had been watching the Holy Staircase he would have been horrified by what happened next.

Martin rose to his feet and walked firmly down the steps, worn into hollows by the knees of many pilgrims. Off he strode, and never looked behind; and as he went he repeated softly to himself the words,

"By faith! by faith!"

DOCTOR MARTIN

VIII

DOCTOR MARTIN

"THERE are two churches, Kunz. I see two spires rising above the houses. Be sure to get the right one!"

"Have no fear, Else. We shall know the Castle Church by the streams of pilgrims going to see the holy relics. Come, this is the way."

The wrinkled features of the old couple beamed with delight as they hastened along the narrow street. Their homespun clothing and toil-worn hands revealed them as hard-working peasants; their dusty shoes told that they had walked many miles on their pilgrimage.

"There are a great many holy relics that the Elector has gathered, are there not?" asked Else as they hurried on.

"More than five thousand!" said Kunz proudly. "Never was there such a collector of relics as our gracious Elector Frederick! He brought back many of them from his pilgrimage to Jerusalem, Father Just told me; but he is getting new ones all the time."

"Shall we know which is St. Elizabeth's hair?" queried Else, dubiously. "That is the one I wish most of all to see; because I was born on her day, and named for her, and I pray to her every day. Can we find it among so many?"

"There will be some one to tell us which it is," said Kunz. "Look, we are almost there! This must be the church."

"Yes," said a man standing near by, "This is the new Castle Church which the Elector has just built. You would not think to see it, that a few years ago there was nothing here but a little building of wood plastered with clay in the cracks, and a pulpit of rough boards! But the Elector does nothing by halves. He has

90

built a church that is worthy of the holy relics."

"This is the place, then, to see the relics?" questioned Kunz.

"Come, I will go with you and show you the way," said the man. "So many come here that the sacristans are always busy and it might be some time before they could attend to you."

The kind stranger piloted the old people safely into the chapel where the relics were kept.

"Here is where you pay your money. Now, this way, friends! Here are the relics; you could not see them all if you stayed for days, but I will show you where some of them are. Here is a tooth of St. Beatrice; here a bone of St. Juliana; these are finger bones of the Holy Innocents, slain by King Herod; here is——"

"Why are you nudging my arm, Else?" inquired Kunz. "Oh, yes, she wants to see the lock of St. Elizabeth's hair, good sir."

"Oh, that is not so distinguished a relic,"

said the man. "It comes from our own part of the country; just over yonder at the Wartburg you know, was the saint's home. Yet she is truly a saint of great power," he added, crossing himself devoutly.

"It is black!" said old Else, in disappointment. "I always imagined that St. Elizabeth had golden hair shining like the sun! And is this truly the hair of my sweet St. Elizabeth? I must say a prayer to her!"

The well-worn rosary slid through the knotted old fingers, as bead after bead was dropped by Else—a bead for every prayer. Kunz stood by with bowed head, and their guide was silent till the old woman's devotions were finished.

"Have you long to stay in Wittenberg?" he asked, as Else arose from her knees.

"We thought of staying several days," said Kunz. "We have friends who live just outside the gates."

"Then you can come here at other times,"

"DO YOU SEE THE PEOPLE THRONGING INTO YONDER DOOR? DR. MARTIN LUTHER IS GOING TO PREACH TO-DAY"

said the man, "and see all the marvelous things at your leisure. Just now there is something else that you ought not to miss. Do you see the people thronging into yonder door? Dr. Martin Luther is going to preach to-day; would you not like to hear him?"

"Dr. Martin Luther!" echoed the old couple.

"Oh, yes!" said Kunz. "Even in our village there are those who have been to hear him, and they say he is a wonderful preacher. Does he preach here all the time?"

"No, he has lately become pastor of the other church here—the Town Church," said their guide. "But right here, in the little old church from the board pulpit, he preached his first sermon some years ago. And as to-day is a festival and the day before the dedication of the new church, he has been asked to preach here. Shall we go in to hear him?"

About two hours later, Kunz and Else

were returning slowly to the gate of the city.

"Did I hear him aright?" asked Kunz, rubbing his puzzled brow. "Why, it sounded as if he meant to say that pilgrimages and relics and all the rest were of no use!"

"He said they often did more harm than good," said old Else, "and that people trusted to them rather than to faith and the love of God."

"If that were so," said Kunz, "then there would be no need to spend money for indulgences, God would forgive us without that. I remember he said, 'Indulgences do nothing but teach people to fear the punishment of sin, instead of the sin itself.'"

"Truly, we know ourselves," said Else, "how wicked George, the blacksmith's son, bought an indulgence for three years, and then came home and robbed his poor old father; and he said he had done no sin, because all the evil he might do in the next three years was already forgiven!"

94

"I wish I knew what to think!" sighed Kunz. "If these sayings are true, we may as well go home and say our prayers to God, instead of praying before the relics of the saints!"

"I am sure he meant every word he said," declared Else. "His bright, dark eyes seemed to look straight into our hearts. He is a good man, I know."

"Here is the gate," said Kunz. "Let us walk a little faster; I am very hungry!"

In the palace of the great Elector, Frederick the Wise, sat two men. One was stout and of middle age, with richly curling beard and princely dress; the other, slender and scholarly, was the court preacher and private secretary of the Elector—George Spalatin, Martin's college friend.

"And what has the bold fellow to say this time?" inquired the Elector, glancing at a letter which Spalatin had just opened.

"He thanks your Grace for the gown

you sent him," said Spalatin, with a smile. "He adds, 'It is of cloth almost too rich for a preacher's robe, were it not the gift of a prince.'"

"Why, the little monk can turn a compliment as well as if he had been brought up in a court," laughed the Elector, not ill pleased. "What else does he say?"

"There are no compliments in the rest of it," said Spalatin, doubtfully.

"I wager not!" said Frederick, stroking his beard. "He is not given to complimenting me or my doings. Yet I am always curious to know what he will say and do next. Read on, George."

"'As to what you write,'" read Spalatin, "'about the most illustrious prince speaking of me frequently and praising me, it does not please me at all. I daily see and experience that those profit me most who speak of me worst. Yet I pray you permit me to thank our prince for his favor and kindness, though I would not be praised by you

96

or any man; for the praise of man is vain, and that of God only is true.' "

"There it is!" said Frederick. "What can you do with a man who would rather have blame than praise? He cared not a bit for my displeasure when he preached two months ago, in my own Castle Church, against relics and indulgences! I have no doubt he will do the same thing again!"

"He is not ungrateful, Your Grace," said Spalatin. "He well knows that it was your Highness who gave the money for his doctor's degree, which he could never have paid himself; and I have not failed to tell him of many other favors from your Grace. But he is far more concerned about the favor of God."

"And he is right!" said the noble Frederick. "Sometimes I think I ought to take a lesson from him. George, tell me now what was in that letter you got from him last spring, which you tried to conceal, and begged me not to ask you to read!"

"Your Grace," began Spalatin in misery; but the Elector clapped him kindly on the shoulder.

"You must and shall tell me! I promise you I will do him no harm. If I am wrong, I can bear to learn it even from a poor teacher in my own university! If I cannot do this, let men no more call me Frederick the Wise!"

Unable to find further argument, Spalatin drew from a hidden pocket in his gown a worn and faded letter.

" 'Many things,' " he read, " 'please your Elector and appear glorious in his eyes, which displease God. I do not deny that the prince is most wise in all worldly matters, but in those which pertain to God and salvation I think he is seven times blind. I do not wish you to conceal this; I am ready to say it to him myself.' "

Spalatin glanced up, in some anxiety. The Elector sat with bowed head, pulling nervously at his beard.

At last he looked up, and there was no anger in his face.

98

"You may go, George," he said gently.
"I wish to be alone and think quietly awhile
on these bold words. What a courage has
the little monk!"

THE SOUND OF HAMMER-BLOWS

Lenoir Rhyne Colley
LIBRARY

IX

THE SOUND OF HAMMER-BLOWS

THE small town of Juterbog was in a great stir one fair morning in the year 1517. Everybody was in festal array and on the main street a procession seemed to be forming.

Here were the magistrates of the little town; the teachers of its schools, leading their scholars; priests, monks, men and women of every degree, carrying candles and garlands. Over their heads waved banners and pennants of every description. It was plain that this was a great occasion.

"Why, good morning, cousin Heinz!" exclaimed a portly citizen, whose dress and the badge he wore proclaimed him a member of the "guild" or union of bakers. "I did not know you were here!"

"I came last night from Wittenberg," said Heinz in reply. "I wanted to see what is going on here."

"Ah, you can't have such grand doings as this in Wittenberg!" laughed the baker. "Is it true that the Elector Frederick has forbidden the sale of indulgences in his dominions?"

"Yes, Fritz, it is true!" replied his cousin. "He wants his people to keep all their money to pay for his own churches and colleges! He has no mind to divide it with the Holy Father at Rome!"

"It matters not to me who gets the money," said Fritz, "whether it is Pope Leo or our own prince, Albert; whether it goes to build St. Peter's Church at Rome, or to pay for making our Albert an archbishop. All I care for is to receive the pardon, and have an easy mind for the rest of my life!"

"For myself," said Heinz, "I think it is very good of the Holy Father to sell thus to us the extra merits of the saints. They do not need them for themselves, and it is a great thing for folks like you and me who are too busy to spend our lives praying and doing deeds of charity, like St. Martin, St. George, and all the rest of them."

"By the way," said Fritz, suddenly reminded of something, "how about your Dr. Martin, over there in Wittenberg? I hear he does not like the selling of pardons."

"He has preached against it several times," said Heinz, grudgingly.

"What would he say, if he knew one of his flock had come twenty miles to meet Friar Tetzel and get an indulgence?" inquired Fritz, laughing.

"It is none of his business!" declared Heinz, defiantly. "But I'll confess to you," he said, in a lower tone, looking around to see that no one else was listening, "that I should not care to go and tell Dr. Martin that I had been here. I am not sure, after all, that I will buy a pardon; I only came to see the procession, and hear what the friar has to say.''

''I must leave you now!'' said Fritz, catching a signal from another of the bakers. ''Our guild is ready to fall in line; the procession is about to move. I will see you again, cousin.''

The banners moved forward; the choristers of the parish church struck up a chant, and the whole company began their march. Yonder on the road was a distant cloud of dust. Friar John Tetzel was coming to set up the sale of pardons in Juterbog.

First out of the dust-cloud appeared a man on horseback, bearing a great red cross. Next came another rider, holding a velvet cushion on which lay a roll of parchment, with a heavy seal hanging from it.

''That is Friar Tetzel's commission from the Holy Father to sell us pardons!'' went around the whisper.

Next was carried upon a wagon a great box, which was full of pardons, ready to be signed with the names of purchasers.

Last, but most important, came the chest in which the money was to be placed.

After all these badges of his office, with other monks in attendance, came the powerful figure of John Tetzel—a man of about sixty, erect and proud, looking about on the people who had come to meet him as a monarch might acknowledge the greetings of his subjects.

The procession from the town, which had taken the side of the road when the red cross drew near, now fell in behind the newcomers, and followed into the village. Over a flower-strewn way, with songs of triumph, the people of Juterbog conducted the seller of pardons into their little city.

Up the street and into the church they went; the first magistrate humbly holding the friar's stirrup while the rider dismounted.

The red cross was set up in front of the high altar; the chest of indulgences was placed beside it. Then Friar Tetzel mounted the pulpit and preached to a crowded house.

As he proceeded, many of his hearers wept and trembled. Dreadful were the pictures he drew of the torments of purgatory. There, he told them, their parents and friends were suffering in the flames, and to give them a chance for rescue he had come this day to Juterbog.

"Lo, heaven is open!" he cried. "When will you enter, if not now? Oh, senseless men, who do not appreciate such a shedding forth of grace, how hard-hearted you are! For twelve pennies you can deliver your father, yet nevertheless you are so ungrateful as not to relieve him in his distress. I tell you that if you have but one garment you should part with it rather than fail of such grace!"

After the sermon the traffic began in earnest. All smiles and bows was Friar Tetzel now.

"This way! just step this way, my dear friends. That is right! Ah, this is a blessed day! As soon as the money tinkles in the

108

chest the soul of your friend will take its flight for Paradise!

"Yes, you can buy an indulgence for your whole life, if you will, and it will keep you out of purgatory in the bargain. Blessed be the saints and our Holy Father, Leo!"

When at last Heinz of Wittenberg passed out of the church door, a fair, new pardon, signed and sealed, reposed in the bosom of his doublet.

He was not the last of Dr. Martin's flock to seek the sign of the red cross, where the eloquent friar "sold grace for gold," as their fearless preacher put it.

In spite of all that Martin Luther could say, many of his people went, secretly or openly, to Juterbog; and few if any came home without an indulgence.

"Why does not Dr. Martin do something?" asked many of his Wittenberg friends as the days went by. "He could hit the traffic a harder blow than it has ever yet received, if he only would. Why does he wait?"

And then, on a misty autumn morning —the 31st of October, 1517—there was an echoing sound of hammer-blows along a quiet street in Wittenberg.

Some of the neighbors peered from their doors to see what caused the noise; but all they saw was the figure of a man, robed in the black gown of a scholar, walking quickly away from the Castle Church; and there, on the church door, was a broad sheet of white.

There was nothing unusual about that. Notices were often posted on the doors of the church; and those who recognized the figure in the black robe only said:

"Dr. Martin has a long notice to post to-day."

But about the time of the afternoon service, held in honor of the Eve of All Saints, there was a different scene about the church door. Students and professors elbowed one another for a chance to read what was written on that white sheet. Townspeople, coming to the service, formed an outer circle, asking curious questions. Here and there,

110

"NO, THERE ARE NINETY-FIVE SUCH STATEMENTS, OR THESES"

a friendly scholar was translating bits of the Latin into German for the benefit of less learned friends.

"The preachers of indulgences are mistaken who say that the Pope's pardon frees a man from all punishment and makes his salvation sure."

"Every Christian who truly repents has full forgiveness of sins, even without letters of pardon."

"Christians are to be taught that he who gives to the poor or lends to one in need does better than he who buys indulgences."

"If the Pope knew how the preachers of indulgences rob the people, he would rather have St. Peter's Church in ashes than have it built with the flesh and bones of his sheep."

"To bring out the truth, Dr. Martin Luther will hold a debate on these questions at Wittenberg. Those who cannot be present, but wish to take part in this debate, are asked to send their opinions by letter."

"Is that all?" demanded a prosperous

111

citizen of his student nephew, who had been interpreting for him.

"No, there are ninety-five such statements, or theses," said the young man. "I tell you, uncle, this will make a stir!"

The student was not mistaken. Within two weeks, all Germany was ringing with the Ninety-five Theses of Dr. Martin Luther, preacher and professor at Wittenberg; and Friar John Tetzel with frowning brow had left his money-chest a little while and was busily penning a reply.

"In four weeks," wrote one of Martin's friends, "the Theses were spread over all Christendom, as though the angels were the postmen."

DR. MARTIN'S BONFIRE

X

DR. MARTIN'S BONFIRE

"WHAT is the matter this morning?" asked the youngest professor of the University of Wittenberg laying down his book in despair.

"Oh, dear Master Philip," spoke up a restless student, "please pardon us! Your lecture is most excellent, but you know we are all excited, and it is hard for us to give attention to-day."

The thin face of Master Philip Melanchthon broke into a smile. He was scarcely as old as many of his pupils, and his slight figure and homely features had been a disappointment to those who saw him when first he came to Wittenberg. But one lecture was enough to make them feel that no more learned man had ever entered among them.

Most of all was Martin Luther drawn to this youth, fourteen years younger than himself, so different in every way from the bold preacher against indulgences.

"I am born to fight with mobs and evil spirits," he often said, "and so my writings are very stormy and warlike. I must remove trees and stumps, cut away thorns and thickets, and fill up quaking bogs. I am the rough woodsman who must blaze the way and clear the path. But Master Philip comes along gently and quietly; builds and plants, sows and waters with joy according to the gifts God has richly bestowed upon him."

Master Philip was beloved by all the students. His lecture-room was always crowded. But Dr. Martin was their hero; and to-day they were all in excitement because of a rumor that was afloat about him.

The students were quick to catch Master Philip's smile.

"Tell us, dear sir," pursued the speaker, "is it true that we are to have a bonfire?"

116

"MASTER PHILIP WAS BELOVED BY ALL THE STUDENTS"

"You will know to-morrow morning!" said the teacher, his face growing grave once more. "But, since all of us are inclined to think of other things, we will dismiss for to-day."

With the roar of a breaking torrent the crowd of eager students surged from the lecture-room.

"It scarcely seems like three years," said Urban Gratz to his friend Franz Spengler, as they left the classroom together, "since we stood around the door of the Castle Church, reading Dr. Martin's great challenge to the pope!"

"How much has happened since then!" replied Franz. "Dr. Martin is now the best known man in all Europe. But he did not think, when he posted his Theses, that he would ever be at strife with the whole Church of Rome!"

"Nor be cast out of it by the pope!" returned Urban. "How he urged us always to be loyal to the head of the Church, and said that surely the pope could not know what his priests and bishops were doing.''

''He thought the Holy Father would surely judge his case justly,'' said Franz, ''but he has found out that there was no justice for him in Rome.''

''Dr. Martin cares little that he has been declared a heretic,'' laughed Urban. ''When this bull of the pope came out, it gave him sixty days to recant his errors. Now six months have passed and he has not taken back a word!''

''What a fuss they have made over him, sending learned doctors and cardinals to change his mind!'' rejoined Franz. ''But this bull makes me angry, little as Dr. Martin cares for it. The decrees of the pope, if he were really a good or wise man, would not condemn without reason.'' And he began to recite the opening sentence of the bull or decree issued by the pope against Martin Luther.

''Arise, Lord, plead thine own cause, arise

118

and protect the vineyard thou gavest Peter from the wild beast who is devouring it.''

"Wild beast!" he quoted, scornfully. "Our Dr. Martin! Never mind, we shall have some fun to-morrow!"

"The students at Leipsic tore the bull to pieces," said Urban. "At Erfurt, they threw it into the water, saying, 'It is only a bubble; let it float!' Here we shall give it to the flames. I hope Dr. Martin himself will do it!"

Next morning the students shouted with joy over the announcement they found posted in Master Philip's handwriting.

"Whoever is devoted to gospel truth, let him be on hand at nine o'clock by the Church of the Holy Cross, outside the walls——"

Most of the readers waited to see no more; they knew well why the summons was given. There was no thought of lectures that day. Long before nine o'clock, streams of townspeople and students went pouring out of the city gate, seeking good places to see what was about to happen.

Already willing hands had brought wood, and had piled upon it the books that contained the laws of the Church of Rome.

"He is coming! Our Doctor is coming!" ran a murmur through the crowd.

Pale but resolute, with set lips and clutching a roll of parchment in his hand, Dr. Martin came from the city gate. Around him were the professors of the University, all in the robes of their office.

The students were ready to cheer, but the grave looks of their teachers held them in check. This was no holiday game, but the defiance of a brave man to a Church that had cast him out for trying to cleanse it of its errors. It might mean life or death for the fearless Doctor, trouble for Wittenberg, and difficulties for its princely master, the Elector Frederick.

Now the little company had arrived at the heap prepared for the burning.

Master Philip, kneeling down, set fire to the wood. The whole assembly seemed to hold its breath. It was so still that all could

120

hear the crackling of the little flames as they rose around the dry fagots. A thin column of blue smoke rose quickly into the frosty December air.

Silently they watched while the fire drew the leathern covers and crisped the edges of the books that lay upon it.

When all was well kindled, Dr. Martin came forward. The pope's decree was unrolled in his hand, the *bulla* or seal that gave it the name of bull dangling close above the flames.

Then the strong, penetrating voice of Martin Luther rose high and clear without a quiver or a break. It was not his own enemy, but that of Christ and the truth which he was about to destroy.

"Because thou hast troubled the Holy One of God," he cried out to the parchment dangling from his hand, "may eternal fire consume thee!"

In another moment, the parchment lay curling and twisting like a living thing among the flames.

Then the students could be restrained no longer. Some one began to sing the great chant of thanksgiving:

"We praise thee, O God!"

Voice after voice caught it up, until the whole company was rolling the melody up to the cloudy winter skies.

Then Dr. Martin and the other professors turned and went back to the city.

All day the excited students went about the town gathering all the books that they could find written by Luther's opponents—of whom there were many—and bringing them to the bonfire, to keep it burning.

The spirit of sport came upon them and they held a mock funeral over the ashes, with chants and orations.

But Dr. Martin spent many hours in prayer. He had attacked the evils in the Church; the Church had cast him out. He had great need of converse with the God in whose name he had made his protest.

122

BEFORE THE GREAT COUNCIL

XI

BEFORE THE GREAT COUNCIL

A CARRIAGE, in which sat four men, was rapidly approaching the imperial city of Worms. After it rode a number of horsemen, and before it advanced a herald, bearing the yellow and black banner of the empire.

"See how the people are pouring from the gate to receive him!" said one of the riders, Dr. Justus Jonas of Wittenberg, to a companion. "Hark! the watchman on the gate sounds a trumpet, to announce his coming to the whole city! Now all the people are leaving their midday meal, and pouring into the streets to see Dr. Martin Luther!"

"He is coming! he is coming!" rose the cry within the city.

"Come, hasten! let us see the great man," exclaimed one citizen to another.

"This is a great day!" replied his neighbor, as they strained their eyes toward the gate. "The man is coming who has taken up the cause of the people against the priests and bishops, yes, against the pope himself! No wonder the whole nation has arisen to stand behind him!"

"Not all!" said a surly voice beside them. "Not all, good neighbor. Archbishop Albert is furious with him; Duke George declares that he shall lose his head. It will be well for the noisy heretic if he returns alive from Worms."

"He has the emperor's promise of safe-conduct!" said the first.

"So had John Huss at Constance," returned the other, "yet they burned him alive! This Luther should be careful how he answers the great and mighty Council."

"See!" said another, pointing to an upper window. "See the pope's ambassador, the wily Aleander, peeping from his window, like a snake from a hole, to see what Dr. Martin looks like."

126

"He dare not come out," said the first speaker. "He is so hated here, since Dr. Martin's books were burned at his insistence, that he would run the risk of being stoned, if he showed himself just now."

"And much good it did to burn them!" said his friend. "The city is full of them again; they are offered for sale even at the doors of the bishop's palace."

"Wait, neighbors," said the surly voice once more. "It may not be books alone that are burned at Worms, before the Diet is over."

"He comes! he comes!" broke out the shouts again, as the banner of the empire came in sight.

Around the corner came the carriage, and halted at the hotel of the Knights of St. John. Out of it stepped a short, dark-haired man in a black gown.

He cast a glance around, with his piercing, dark eyes. The throng pressed to touch his garments.

Up at the housetops he looked; down the

street and up again. Every door, every window, was crowded with gazing faces.

"God be with me!" exclaimed Martin Luther, feeling suddenly that the eyes of all Germany, yes, of all Europe, were upon him.

Then, turning quickly, he passed into his hotel.

That evening came his friend, George Spalatin, the Elector's secretary, to greet Dr. Martin.

"Thank God that you have arrived in safety!" he exclaimed, greeting Martin with warm affection.

"Our journey has been safe and prosperous, dear George," returned Dr. Martin, brightly.

"He speaks very mildly of his triumphal procession," said Dr. Jonas, laughing. "At every city and hamlet he was met by marching and singing people, cheering him on his way.

"When we came near Erfurt the whole town poured out to welcome him. Professors, students, citizens, all came flocking out.

Dr. Eoban Hess, one of his old college mates, had prepared a poem in his honor; another delivered an oration.

"We stayed there over Sunday; and another good friend of Dr. Martin's, Prior John Lange, asked him to preach for him. The church was so crowded that one of the galleries cracked, and the people thought it was going to break down. But Dr. Martin cried out to them to have no fear, and quieted them; then he went on and finished his sermon.

"Everywhere the people begged him not to come to Worms.

"'Your life is not safe, dear Dr. Martin. Do not go on,' was the cry on every hand. But he answered,

"'Though there were as many devils in Worms as there are tiles on the houseroofs, I would still go on!'"

"Yes," replied Spalatin, "I myself was afraid, and sent him a message to turn back; but his faith and courage make me ashamed to fear. The Elector is here, and will stand by his professor and his university to the utmost of his power.''

''I have a stronger Friend than the great Elector, dear George,'' put in Martin with a quiet smile.

Next day the summons came for Martin to appear before the great Diet, or council of the empire, which was holding its sessions in the bishop's palace.

The streets were so thronged that the imperial herald was not able to get Dr. Martin safely through the crowd; they were obliged to go back into the hotel garden and so make their way to the garden of the palace.

Into the great hall the herald led the solitary, black-robed figure. Within sat waiting for him all the nobles and princes of the empire.

Just as the doors were opened, the gray-bearded old general, George of Frundsberg, stepped to his side and slapped him on the shoulder.

''Little monk, little monk!'' he said kindly,

130

"you are about to go into a more terrible battle than I and my knights have ever fought; but if your cause is just, and God is with you, go forward boldly, and have no fear!"

And from all around came cries of encouragement.

"Play the man! Fear not!"

From the crowd outside, and the people in the streets, arose shouts that could be heard within the palace.

"Luther, our Luther!" "God bless Dr. Martin!"

So he went in, with smiling lips, to face the brilliant assembly.

On the throne chair, in his robes of state, sat the young emperor, Charles the Fifth. His long, pale face was calm as marble; but as his eyes fell on the slight figure following the herald a sneer crossed his cold lips. Turning to the nobles beside him he said disdainfully,

"Is that the monk? He will never make a heretic of me!"

All about him gathered the princes of his realm—archbishops, cardinals, electors, margraves, dukes, and landgraves; beside these, the ambassadors of all the principal rulers of Europe.

Among them all Dr. Martin saw but one face he could count friendly—the broad, good-natured countenance of the wise Elector Frederick. Cold and hostile looks were plenty; and among them the dark, crafty face of the pope's ambassador, Aleander, cast on him such a look of hatred that he said to himself:

"So must Annas and Caiaphas have looked on my Lord and Master!"

"What terrible eyes he has!" thought Aleander, shrinking from the keen gaze. "I wish he would not look at me!"

Beside the throne stood a table with books upon it. As Luther glanced toward it, he saw the titles of several of his own books.

Then the voice of the chancellor broke the silence.

"Martin Luther, his imperial majesty has
132

summoned you here, that you may recant and recall the words you have written in these books, published by you and spread abroad.

"First, do you confess that these books, having your name on the title-page, were written by you?

"Second, will you recall and retract what you have said in them, or will you reaffirm what is written therein?"

"Let the titles of the books be read!" cried a voice.

As the names of the books were read, one after another, Luther bowed his head, assenting to each. At the close, he spoke.

"I cannot deny that I have written all the books named; and I have also written some others not mentioned here.

"As to the other question, it is too grave to be answered in a word; for, not having considered what I am to reply, I might not answer wisely, and might utter either more or less than the exact truth.

"Therefore, I beg that your Imperial

133

Majesty will give me time to consider, that I may answer the question without denying my Lord or losing my own soul."

There was a buzz of excited conversation among the councilors. The Italian ambassadors did not want delay; the heretic had spoken in a low voice, and they believed that he was frightened and ready to recant if he were threatened.

At length the chancellor announced that a delay of twenty-four hours should be granted; and the herald led Martin back to his room at the inn.

"HERE I STAND"

XII

"FRIGHTENED? not at all!" declared Justus Jonas next day to the friends who besieged the hotel all the morning. "You will hear whether he is frightened when he is ready to give his answer!"

"But why did he not answer at once?" asked one impatient noble.

"Dear sir," said Dr. Jonas, "he wanted to consult a Friend."

"What friend?" exclaimed the noble in surprise. "Surely Dr. Martin needs no one to tell him what to say! Did he consult a lawyer, so that he might be sure of saying nothing his enemies might turn against him?"

"All night," said Dr. Jonas, in a lower tone, "all night we have heard Dr. Martin's voice, in his room, talking with his Friend.

"'O thou, my God!' we heard him say, 'stand by me against the wisdom of the world! It is thy cause, not mine. For mine own honor I am not concerned; with these great men of the world I have nothing to do. I am ready to sacrifice my life, as patiently as a lamb. But the cause is thine; thou must help me to defend it!'"

The nobleman's voice was husky, as he turned away.

"God grant it!" he said.

Once more, late in the afternoon, the herald came to conduct Dr. Martin before the Diet. The crowd in the streets was greater than ever, and again they made their way through the gardens to the palace.

"How cheerful he looks!" said the watchers in the palace court, as Martin passed into the building.

"Perhaps he has made up his mind to recant," said one. "He knows he is safe."

The hall was so crowded that the princes had difficulty in getting to their seats. Aleander was not present. He said that the pope's ambassador could not demean himself by hearing a heretic speak. Probably the "terrible eyes" of the lonely monk had more to do with his absence.

Again the chancellor called on Dr. Martin to recant. His words were bitter and threatening; but they made no change in the serene look on the face of the accused.

Then Martin Luther began to speak. All hesitation was gone from his manner. His head was raised, and his ringing voice reached every corner of the crowded hall.

"Most serene Lord and Emperor," he began, "most illustrious princes, most clement lords——"

The throng grew still as death to listen. The April twilight was darkening, and torches had been lighted to illuminate the hall. The heat grew intense; yet no one stirred, while Dr. Martin spoke on and on.

"My books are of three kinds," he said. "Some are works on pious subjects, to which no objection can be made by any one. Some are attacks on the power of the pope and the many evils in the Church; these I cannot retract, without denying the doctrine of Christ. The third kind are those in which I have answered those who have written against me; in these I may have been too severe, and have made some mistakes in the way of speaking too violently.

"But, if any one can show me anything in any of my writings which is false and contrary to the Word of God, I am ready to throw my books into the fire with my own hands!"

"Speak to the point, Luther! Will you, or will you not recant?" cried the chancellor.

Then Martin, his deep eyes glowing like stars, flung back the immortal answer:

"Unless I am convinced, by the Holy Scriptures—not by the word of popes and councils, for they may be in error—but by the Word of God himself, by which alone my conscience is bound, I neither can nor will recant anything!"

A tumult of voices arose. The chancellor

140

"HERE I STAND. I CANNOT DO OTHERWISE"

began to argue, the princes to interrupt. Out
of the midst of the din once more arose the
voice of Martin Luther, clear and firm as an
angel's trumpet:

"Here I stand. I cannot do otherwise.
God help me! Amen!"

Then the young emperor arose, dismissing
the Diet. The assembly poured out of the
hall, pushing and thronging so that several
of the imperial guards had to be sent to Martin's side, to lead him safely through the
crowd.

As he passed out of the doors, with a
guard on either side, the nobles in the court
cried out,

"He is arrested! they are taking him to
prison!"

"They are taking me to my hotel," called
out Martin, and the crowd was pacified.

Across the palace yard and into that of
the hotel he was led, to the inn where his
waiting friends had spent the anxious hours.

"I am through! I am through!" cried

Martin exultingly, with uplifted hands, as they rushed to meet him.

"You have retracted nothing, dear Dr. Martin?" cried his faithful friend, Nicholas Amsdorf.

"Retracted?" exclaimed Martin, with the ring of victory in his voice. "Even though I had a hundred heads, I would have had them all cut off before I would have retracted anything!"

The traveling carriage in which Dr. Martin and his companions sat was rolling slowly along a forest road not far from the town of Eisenach. Martin had been spending the last few days in visiting the scenes of his boyhood. He had just left the home of his aged grandmother in the little village of Mora. Of his traveling companions none were left but Nicholas Amsdorf and a monk from Wittenberg named Petzenstein.

"Well, Dr. Martin, we shall soon be in Wittenberg again; and what then?" asked the monk, as they journeyed along.

"Yes; what then?" laughed Dr. Martin, in reply.

"You do not seem to consider, Brother Martin, that the emperor is about to declare you an outlaw!" continued the monk.

"Yes, brother, I know it well enough," said Martin. "I think I have heard all the points of that decree on which Aleander and the emperor are so busy. My books are all to be burned, and no more are to be published, sold, or read. I am to be seized wherever found and handed over to the emperor for justice. All men are forbidden to give me food or shelter or to aid me in any way. I am a condemned heretic, a man outside of the law! How happy the pope will be!"

"You take it very lightly, Brother Martin," said the monk, gloomily.

"My cause is in good hands," said Martin cheerily. "One who is stronger than pope or emperor has cared for me and will not leave me now!"

The twilight came on early under the dense

143

leafage of the forest. Still the horses plodded on. The monk was plainly nervous, and Amsdorf now and then cast uneasy glances on either side; but Dr. Martin's face was cheerful and serene, and his talk betrayed no fear.

Suddenly a sound of galloping hoofs smote their ears. Before the sleepy driver of the carriage could do more than look around, five horsemen, wearing masks, barred the way.

"Robbers!" cried the monk, in terror, leaping from the carriage, and making off into the woods.

To him the horsemen paid little attention; nor yet to Amsdorf, who was not so greatly alarmed.

With a show of force, they dragged the driver from his seat.

"Be still!" said one of the masked men to him with a threatening gesture. "We will do you no harm. We want nobody but Dr. Martin Luther."

Martin was already standing up in the car-

144

"WE WANT NOBODY BUT DR. MARTIN LUTHER"

riage. With no resistance he allowed his captors to throw about him the long cloak of a knight, and lead him away into the forest, where a haltered horse awaited him.

"On again to Wittenberg!" commanded Nicholas Amsdorf, when the highwaymen had vanished with their prize. "We must go and tell them that Dr. Martin has been seized and carried off. May God keep him in safety!"

"KNIGHT GEORGE"

XIII

"KNIGHT GEORGE"

SPRING had passed into summer and summer into autumn. Now the snows of winter were bending the great trees around the high castle of Wartburg, crowning the lofty hill above the town of Eisenach.

One December day, before the early shadows had begun to fall, a man on horseback might have been seen ascending the steep path to the castle. The road was partly broken, but in places where the snow had drifted he was obliged to dismount and lead his horse around.

Mounting again, after one of these excursions from the way, he caught sight of a figure moving under the leafless trees. Riding forward a little farther, he halted to look more closely.

It was a man in the garb of a knight, with a sword belted to his side and a dark cloak hanging from his shoulders. A thick, black beard covered the lower part of his face; above it sparkled eyes at once kind and keen.

When the eyes glanced toward the road and perceived the rider sitting his horse like a statue, the knight turned, scattering with a hasty gesture the remainder of the crumbs with which he had been feeding a little flock of snowbirds.

"Is it you, my dear George?" he cried. "Have you come at last to see me?"

"Martin, is it really you?" queried George Spalatin, still looking dubiously at the knightly figure.

"No, no!" laughed the black-bearded man. "Martin is not known about here. To all but the lord of the castle I am Knight George, paying a long visit to Wartburg."

Spalatin dismounted and threw the bridle over his arm. Together the two friends walked slowly up the winding path toward the castle.

150

"TO ALL BUT THE LORD OF THE CASTLE I AM KNIGHT GEORGE"

"First you will go, of course, to the good knight of the castle," said Martin. "Then come to my room, for I have many things to say to you in private."

Several hours later, they sat in the December dusk with no other light than that of a wood-fire crackling merrily, in an upper chamber of a small building apart from the main body of the castle.

"This is a safe and quiet retreat you have chosen for me, George," said Martin, "or I should say, our gracious master the Elector for I guessed all along that he was at the bottom of the plan to hide me away, though you tell me he would not for a long time allow you to tell him where I was."

"It is a safe retreat, while you stay in it, Martin," said Spalatin, rather severely. "But you show too much anxiety to be out of it; and that is why I have come here in the middle of winter."

"Oh! so you know I have been to Wittenberg!" said Martin serenely. "It was only for three days, George; I did not even go

151

near my lodgings, but spent the time in the house of Nicholas Amsdorf; and you know I was well disguised. Why, you yourself, when you came just now, hardly knew me in this beard!"

"It was too great a risk,'' said Spalatin, shaking his head. "All the country rang with the sudden disappearance of Martin Luther; and spies have been busy ever since to discover your whereabouts. You will be caught; and then you know what to expect."

"Dear friend," said Martin, gravely, "there are many troubles at Wittenberg and I felt that I must go and help to quiet them. Perhaps before long I shall go back to stay; I must, if I am needed."

"Then you go at your own risk," said Spalatin abruptly.

"I shall not ask the Elector to protect me," returned Martin. "I shall go under a far higher protection than his!

"But now, dear George, be not angry with me. I have surely been patient and quiet all these months, even when I was ready to die

152

of idleness. I have roamed the woods gathering wild strawberries in summer and nuts in autumn; I have even tried to engage in the pleasures of the chase with the knights of the castle, and have decided that these sports of the nobility are not for a plain doctor like me!"

"Did you not enjoy the hunting?" inquired Spalatin, his face relaxing into a smile.

"A bitter-sweet pleasure!" said Dr. Martin. "We caught two hares and three poor little partridges—a fine occupation for men of leisure!

"One poor little hare came running to me, as if it would ask me to save it. I hid it in my sleeve, and stood aside; but the dogs smelt it out, and bit it through my coat, breaking its leg. I have had enough of such hunting!"

"But you had books," said Spalatin.

"Yes, and wrote them!" said Martin. "I have been busy enough at that. The trouble

153

is that you and the Elector want to stop me; my writings are too bold for you."

"There are only a few we want to keep back," said Spalatin. "Here you are writing about the vows of the monks being of no effect; and over there at Wittenberg your monks are leaving the monastery and exciting the people by trying to take up other occupations. If all the monks leave their houses and go out to become tradesmen, how shall the poor weavers and bakers and merchants live any more?"

"I must say what is the truth, George," said Martin, "no matter what comes of it. I was a monk myself, and am set free from that bondage by the grace of God. I know now that it is not his will that men should leave the common path of life to serve him. I have dedicated my book on the vows of monks to my good old father, who told me from the first that they were wrong.

"But now, George, I have a plan which may suit you better. We talked it over at Wittenberg."

154

"What is that?" asked Spalatin.

"George," said Dr. Martin, drawing his chair nearer to his friend, "I have taken many of the old beliefs away from the people.

"I have told them that masses and pilgrimages, relics and indulgences, prayers to the saints and to the Virgin Mary, are all of no use.

"I have taught them that the priests and the bishops are not to be followed unless they speak the truth of God. I have broken the chains in which they were held and freed them from obedience to the pope.

"I have told them, over and over, that they need no man or saint to stand between them and their Father in heaven.

"But how shall they worship him whom they do not know? How shall they know him, except through his own Word?

"You know that the priests have tried to keep the people from reading God's Word for themselves. Even among the learned, few know the Bible as they should; and the common people cannot read it because they know no Latin. It is true that some have tried to put the Word of God into our language; but these translations are full of errors, and they are not in simple words that common folks can understand."

"You mean——" said Spalatin.

"I mean," said Dr. Martin, "that I am beginning to put the New Testament into such German as the mother uses in the home, the child in the street, the common man in the market-place. I mean that I am going to put the Bible in their own speech into the hands of the people of Germany!"

"Martin," said Spalatin, "this is a great undertaking! Will not the poor and humble be too ignorant to understand even in such language the great truths of the Bible?"

"You speak like a priest!" said Martin, vigorously. "God will make his Word plain. 'The entrance of thy word giveth light.' That is the promise!"

THE STRANGER AT THE BLACK BEAR

XIV

THE STRANGER AT THE BLACK BEAR

TWO young men were traveling along a muddy road in a pelting thunderstorm.

"We are almost at Jena now, Walter," said the elder of the two. "There we shall find shelter."

"Yes, here is the gate!" said the other. "How glad I shall be to get out of the storm!"

Into the streets they passed, and began to inquire for lodgings. From inn to inn they went, but nowhere could find entertainment; and all the time the rain came pitilessly down.

"There seems to be no place for us, John," said Walter anxiously. "Shall we not go out again and try to find shelter in some village or farmhouse?"

To the gate they turned again; and just beneath it they ran almost into a well-dressed citizen, standing under the arch to wait for a lull in the tempest.

"Where are you going, friends, in such a storm?" he inquired kindly.

"We are going to seek lodging in the country, sir," replied John.

"It is very late," said the man, with fatherly interest. "The night will come on before you can reach the nearest village; and in this driving rain you may easily miss the road. Would it not be better to stay in the city to-night?"

"Dear sir," said John, "we called at all the inns to which we were directed, but everywhere we were turned away, and could get no lodging. We must go farther, for we cannot sleep out in the rain."

"Have you tried the Black Bear?" asked the good man.

"Where is that, sir? We did not see it."

"Just outside the city," was the reply.

"Look this way; you can see the lights twinkling through the mist."

"Thank you, thank you, kind sir!" exclaimed the young man. "Come, Walter, we will hasten on!"

At the inn of the Black Bear, the drenched and shivering travelers were met by the landlord at the door.

"Yes, I have room for you," he said hospitably. "Come in, come in, and dry yourselves at the fire."

In the guest-room of the inn a man sat reading at the table. He looked up as the landlord opened the door.

"Come in and sit down with me, friends," he said heartily. "Ah, you have been drenched in the storm!"

The two young men entered bashfully.

"We are not fit to sit at the table with you, sir," said John. "We are covered with mud. We will sit here on a bench by the door."

"You will do nothing of the sort," he said, closing his book. "You will come to the table, and the landlord will bring something to warm your chilled bones and keep you from taking cold."

Modestly the travelers took their seats near the stranger. He was dressed in the costume of a knight, a red leather cap, hose and doublet, and a sword by his side.

"How his deep eyes sparkle!" whispered Walter to John. "I can hardly bear to look into them!"

"You are Swiss," began the stranger, noting the dress of the young men. "From what part of Switzerland do you come?"

"From St. Gall," replied the elder. "I am John Kessler,* and this is my friend, Walter Brun. We are going to Wittenberg."

"Ah!" said he; "at Wittenberg you will find some good countrymen of yours, Dr. Jerome Schurf and his brother Augustine."

"Can you tell us, sir," asked Walter eagerly, "whether Martin Luther is now at Wittenberg?"

"I have good reason to believe," said the man, "that Luther is not now at Wittenberg

* A real name. That of his friend is invented.

162

but will soon be there. But Dr. Philip Melanchthon is there; he teaches Greek, and there are others who teach Hebrew. I would advise you to study both of these languages, for they will help you greatly in understanding the Holy Scriptures."

"Thank God!" said Kessler fervently. "We are both resolved, if our lives are spared, to see and hear Dr. Luther. Indeed, it is on his account that we are taking this journey."

"How is that?" asked their companion.

"Both of us," said John Kessler, "have been brought up from boyhood by our parents to be priests. Now we understand that Luther wants to overturn the priesthood, and we want to hear what he has to say about it."

"Oh!" said he. "And what do they think of Luther in Switzerland?"

"Some thank God," said John, "that through him God's truth has been revealed; others, especially the priests, call him a terrible heretic."

163

"Ah, yes, the priests, of course!" said the man, with a smile.

Meantime, Walter had picked up the book which the stranger had laid on the table and showed it silently to his friend. It was a copy of the Psalms in Hebrew! More and more the young men wondered who this man could be.

Just then the landlord came to the door and beckoned to Kessler to come out.

"I perceive," he said, "that you would like to see and hear Luther. Well, it is he who is sitting and talking with you!"

"Oh, come, Mr. Landlord," said John, taking it as a joke, "you are making sport of me."

"No, it is really he," said the innkeeper, "but do not act as if you knew him."

John hastened back into the room and made an excuse to draw Walter to one side and tell him what the landlord had said.

"Oh, no, John!" said Walter. "Surely you are mistaken! Did not the landlord say 'Hutten'? The names sound somewhat alike. Perhaps it is the brave and learned knight, Ulrich von Hutten.''

"Well, perhaps he did," said John uncertainly. "It could hardly be Dr. Luther in such a garb!"

Presently two merchants came in to spend the night. One of them laid on the table an unbound book.

"What book is that?" asked the stranger.

"It is Dr. Luther's explanation of some of the Gospels and Epistles, which has just been printed," said the merchant. "Have you seen it?"

"I shall soon," was the knight's reply, which made the students look at each other again.

Now the landlord called them all to supper. Again the students protested that they were not fit to sit with the others, and asked to have something at a table apart.

"Come on! come on!" said the knight. "Sit down here with us! I am going to pay for your supper."

All through the meal, students and merchants could scarcely eat for listening to the stranger's delightful conversation.

After supper, when the merchants went out to see to their horses, John said to the knight,

"You have done us great honor and great kindness, noble sir. We never expected to sit at a table with the famous Hutten."

The stranger laughed merrily. Just then the landlord came in, and the knight said to him,

"I have become a nobleman to-night, for these Swiss imagine that I am Ulrich von Hutten!"

"You are not he, but Martin Luther!" said the landlord, seeing his good humor.

"They take me for Hutten, you for Luther!" laughed the stranger. "Whom shall I be next?"

He rose, threw his cloak over his shoulder, and said to the puzzled students,

"When you reach Wittenberg, give my regards to Dr. Jerome Schurf."

166

"Willingly," said Kessler, "if we knew what name to give him!"

"Say only," said the stranger, " 'He who is to come sends greetings.' "

The students went their way next morning toward Wittenberg. The next Saturday, they called on Dr. Schurf to present their letters of introduction.

There sat the stranger, looking just as they had seen him in the guest-room of the Black Bear!

"You are really Martin Luther!" exclaimed John Kessler, in delight.

A great laugh arose from all the friends assembled in the room—Dr. Philip, Justus Jonas, Amsdorf, and others.

Martin himself laughed most heartily of all; and pointing to Melanchthon, said, "This is Dr. Philip, of whom I told you. Welcome to Wittenberg, dear fellow travelers."

Dr. Martin had come back to stay. The Wartburg could hold him no longer; there was too much to do at Wittenberg!

167

"LORD KATIE"

XV

"LORD KATIE"

"IS Mistress Cranach at home?" asked a morning visitor, standing at the door of Master Lucas Cranach, the noted artist of Wittenberg.

"Yes, Mistress Katie!" said the little maid. "Will you please come in?" and, leading the guest through the long corridor, she announced the arrival by opening a door, and saying, "Here is Mistress Katherine Luther!"

The wife of Lucas Cranach rose, with both hands extended, to greet with pleasure a familiar and welcome guest.

"How are you, dear Katie?" she said. "I did not expect to see you so early; but then, you are always up with the birds! No wonder Dr. Martin calls you 'The Morning Star of Wittenberg,' because you always rise before the sun.''

"It was market morning, you know," said Mistress Katie, removing her cloak. "I wished to go early, so that I could get here before Dr. Martin had finished the sitting he was to give Master Lucas for his portrait. I have sent the little maid home with the basket, and now I will talk with you and wait for him."

As she spoke she picked up a piece of the mending with which Mistress Cranach was busy, and without ceremony began to work on it.

Mistress Katie was dressed in the usual morning costume of a German housewife— white cap and kerchief over a dark woolen dress with close-fitting sleeves and full skirt.

Her auburn hair was parted smoothly and almost hidden under the ample folds of the cap. Her dark-blue eyes were quick and glancing; her rather plain face was both shrewd and kindly. She was almost thirty years of age.

"HERE IS MISTRESS KATHERINE LUTHER"

"How much better Dr. Martin is looking, Katie," remarked her friend, as their busy fingers made the needles fly. "He is not the same man since his marriage. Truly, you take good care of him!"

"And no light task it is," laughed Dr. Martin's wife. "If you could see how hard it is to get him to dinner when he is busy with his writing! That is partly the reason I came to wait for him to-day; I have fresh greens for dinner, and if he and Master Lucas get to talking, or if he comes home, slips into his study, and locks the door, the greens may stand till they are spoiled, though he really is very fond of them!"

"His whole heart is in his work," said Mistress Cranach, smiling. "I can imagine that he often forgets his meals."

"Before we were married," said Katie, "he says he had no regular meal-times, but went and got something to eat when he happened to think of it, unless he was invited out to dine. No wonder he was hardly ever well! Even yet he has severe spells of illness

173

at times. He has never taken care of himself, or thought of his own health, in all his
life."

"Then it is high time some one did it for
him," said her friend. "But I can guess
that it is not easy to train him into regular
habits."

"You should have seen the house when I
came into it!" said Katie. "He hardly
ever made his bed properly, but left it open
so that it would be easier to get into. His
papers and books were littered about everywhere, and he makes a terrible outcry even
now if they are disturbed. His little dog
used to make a bed in his papers, and often
chewed them up, as well as his boots and
leather belts!

"I keep the dog outside, clean up as much
as I dare, and shut my eyes to the heaps of
papers! But he knows he is much more
comfortable, though he doesn't like to be disturbed by sweeping and dusting."

"He has no care for little things," said
Mistress Cranach.

174

"No, nor greater things, sometimes," said Mistress Katie. "He would give away everything we have in the house if I did not watch him! Let any poor student come with a tale of wo, and Dr. Martin gives him the last penny in his purse! He gives away his clothing, the food from the table, and the gold and silver dishes that our friends gave us when we were married.

"The other day, one of his friends invited him to his marriage. Dr. Martin could not go, but he wrote him a letter, saying,

" 'I am sending you as a gift a large silver vase which was given to us and which I hope you will accept in token of our love and good wishes.'

"The letter lay open on the table, and he was called away before it was finished. I suspected he had some such plan, for I saw him casting looks at the vase while he wrote. So I put it away.

"When he came back, the vase was gone! He looked at me, and laughed; then he put a postscript to his letter.

175

" 'I am sorry I cannot send you the vase, after all; because my Lord Katie, who rules me and my household, has hidden it away!' "

"That is right, Katie," said her friend, approvingly. "He would beggar himself and you if you did not look after such things. He is the greatest man in Germany, but he is like a child when it comes to matters of money. We knew that long ago. He never thinks of himself."

"He is the best and greatest man in the world," declared his wife, the quick tears starting to her keen eyes. "Were it not for him and the books he wrote I should still be a lonely nun in the convent at Nimbschen."

"You were not meant for a nun, dear Katie," said Mistress Cranach. "Some women might have been happy in such a life, though since we have known Dr. Martin we believe that it is not the right way to please God, but you have the talents of a house-wife and a man of business as well!"

"I never could spend my time in a little cell even at the convent," said Katie. "I

176

used to beg the abbess to let me go out and help to manage things on the estate of the convent—to oversee the farming, the buying and selling of cattle, the weaving and bleaching of linen, and all the rest; and she found I was much better indoors when I had been busy outside for a while.

"I would never have chosen to be a nun; but my mother died when I was a little girl, and my father sent me to be brought up in the convent. When Dr. Luther's books came out, we managed to get some and read them. When I read the one on the vows of monks and nuns, I felt as if some one had opened the door of a prison, and called me out into the bright sunshine! You know the rest, dear friend—how twelve of us escaped, and nine came to Wittenberg; how the good people here received and sheltered us; how good Mistress Reichenbach gave me a home, until Dr. Martin asked me to be his wife. I owe everything to him."

"What is this?" interrupted a merry

voice. "Lord Katie here, and talking about me, as usual. What sermons these women preach! Their tongues are never still!"

And Dr. Martin entered, with his handsome and stately friend, the artist Cranach.

"Never was such a manager as my Lord Katie," continued Dr. Martin jestingly. "She has made me dig a garden, and plant lilies and roses as well as things to eat. Now we are making a fish-pond, and soon we shall have fish for our table.

"She takes students to board, and lays money aside. Presently we are going to buy a little farm which she can manage to her heart's content.

"She is like the virtuous woman in the Proverbs; she rises while it is yet dark, she plants a vineyard, she works willingly with her hands, and eats not the bread of idleness!

"It is true, she interrupts me sometimes by asking questions, or calling me to dinner when I am busy writing; but," he added, dropping his bantering tone, "she is a true

178

helpmate to me, and I thank God for her.''

And while the happy tears dimmed Katie's blue eyes, Master Lucas, stroking his long beard, replied,

"You have proved the truth, dear Dr. Martin, of the Scripture which says, 'Whoso findeth a wife findeth a good thing, and obtaineth favor from the Lord.'"

179

WIDENING CIRCLES

XVI

THE living-room in the old monastery, abandoned now by all the monks and for many happy years the home of Dr. Martin Luther and his family, was all aglow, and ringing with sounds which would have astonished the prior and the brothers who once dwelt there.

In the midst of the room stood an evergreen tree, bedecked with toys and candles. Hans Luther, aged nine, was buried in the pages of a new book. Martin, junior, a rosy boy of five, jumping up and down in glee under the spicy branches, was blowing with all his might on a toy trumpet.

Quiet, dainty Magdalene, his six-year-old sister, was sitting on the floor, rocking a new doll in a tiny cradle, and trying to sing it a cradle-song, sadly interrupted by the blasts of the trumpet.

Paul, aged two, sat in a corner, examining the construction of a wooden horse; and Baby Margaret, in her mother's arms, crowed in delight, and stretched her little arms to catch the glittering balls that adorned the Christmas tree; while "Auntie Lena," or Magdalene von Bora, Katherine Luther's aunt, held up a gaily colored rattle, shaking it to attract the baby's attention.

Into the midst of this happy group walked three men in doctors' gowns, smiling as they saw the pretty picture under the green boughs.

"Father! Father has come back!" shouted Martin, flinging himself bodily on the first of the newcomers.

"Yes, the sick girl I went to see is better," said Dr. Martin, with a nod to Katie. "And look whom I have brought with me! Dr. Jonas, and——"

"Dr. Philip!" cried the boy, running up

to the frail, gentle man in the fur-lined robe, whom all the children loved as one of the family. "See my horn! You may blow it, if you want to!"

Little Magdalene came shyly to lay her doll in Dr. Philip's hand. He sat down and lifted the little girl to his knee, where she nestled until her father sat down, with the baby laughing and jumping in his arms. Then she slid quietly off, and went over to her father, leaning against his knee without a word, till he noticed her presence, and put his arm around her.

"It is growing late," said Mistress Katie, "but the children would not hear of going to bed till you had come home, so that we could sing our Christmas carols together."

"Well, well," said Dr. Martin, "take the baby, then, Katie, till I get my lute, and we will end the day as it should be ended."

Book, trumpet, and toy horse were laid aside; the doll was tucked tenderly in its cradle, and the little group, gathering around Dr. Martin, sang carol after carol, even the children chirping the melodies, if sometimes uncertain about the words.

"Sing *our* songs, father!" begged Hans, in a pause; and, smiling, the father led them in one of the simple Christmas hymns he had composed for them:

"Away in a manger, no crib for his bed,
  The little Lord Jesus laid down his sweet head;
  The stars in the bright sky looked down where he lay,
  The little Lord Jesus, asleep in the hay."

"Sing about the cradle, father, dear!" whispered Magdalene, rocking her doll gently; and so they sang another of Dr. Martin's sweet songs:

"Yet were the world ten times as wide,
    With gold and jewels beautified,
    It would be far too small to be
    A narrow cradle, Lord, for thee

"Ah, dearest Jesus, holy Child,
    Make thee a bed, soft, undefiled,
    Within my heart, that it may be
    A quiet chamber kept for thee!"

186

"TAKE THE BABY, THEN, KATIE, TILL I GET MY LUTE, AND WE WILL END
THE DAY AS IT SHOULD BE ENDED"

At the last note, laying the lute aside, the father knelt by his chair. Hans promptly dropped beside him; Magdalene slipped to her knees by the tiny cradle, and folded the doll's hands before she clasped her own. All the rest knelt also, except the mother, on whose lap Baby Margaret had fallen asleep, and who sat with head bowed over her little one.

With words as simple and tender as the songs they had just been singing, the father commended them all for the night to the care of God, who had sent his dear Son to be the world's Christmas gift.

"Now, Katie, take these sleepy little folks to bed!" commanded Dr. Martin, as they rose from their knees. "Philip, Jonas, and I will sit here and talk a little while. Good night, my Hans; good night, dear little Magdalene; good night, Martin and Paul!"

And the drowsy procession trooped away to happy dreams.

"What a delightful evening!" said Philip, his thin face beaming with pleasure, as he waved a last good night to little Magdalene.

"You would not think you were in the house of a condemned heretic and outlaw, would you, dear Philip?" said Dr. Martin, with a short laugh. "Often I wonder how it is that a man with a price on his head should dare to be merry and live in such security; and I can only say that it is the Lord's doing."

"And that of the princes who took our side," said blunt Justus Jonas. "So many came over to us, even at Worms, that the emperor's ban was dead before it was issued!"

"Truly," said Philip, "the princes have been loyal! I shall never forget, at Augsburg, when we were about to present the Confession of our faith to the Diet there, how I urged that it should be signed only by us doctors and preachers, who were already so deep in the matter that it could not hurt us to be still deeper.

"Then our noble Elector, John the Constant—who came out far more openly on our

188

"YOU WOULD NOT THINK YOU WERE IN THE HOUSE OF A CONDEMNED HERETIC AND OUTLAW"

side than even the Elector Frederick did—
said,

"'Not so, Philip! I, too, will confess my
Christ!'

"Then the seven princes signed the Confession of Augsburg, and showed to all the
world what the faith is in which we stand."

"I never felt the weight of the emperor's
ban so heavily as at that time!" said Dr.
Martin. "How I longed to be with you at
Augsburg! Yet I dared not go into the emperor's presence, but could go only as far
as Coburg, and sit there and wait for news
from the Diet!"

"It was indeed a great occasion for us,"
said Philip, "but, though you were not there,
you were still the center and the soul of it
all! For who but you has been our leader,
from the day you nailed that paper of yours
on the door of the Castle Church?

"Sometimes I imagine," continued Philip,
thoughtfully, "that I see this great move-
ment, the Reformation, as men call it,
spreading out like circles on still water,

189

widening and widening till they reach the farthest shores of earth.

"Already it has spread to France, England, Switzerland, and the northern lands. Ever the circles widen; everywhere men called of God are taking up the work, proclaiming liberty of conscience, and the free Word of God.

"But the source and center of it is here at Wittenberg; just like the stone thrown into the water, from whence the ripples spread. And the stone—the first word of protest—was thrown by Martin Luther!"

"People begin to call us 'Protestants' now," remarked Jonas.

"Yes," said Philip, "but we do not merely denounce evils. A 'protest' means a witnessing for something. We witness for the truth of God."

"And for the Word of God in the hands and in the lives of all men," said Dr. Martin, quickly. "Sometimes I think, Philip, that the greatest work you and I have ever done, and that for which the world will thank us

190

TRANSLATING THE BIBLE

Melanchthon   Luther   Pomeranus   Cruciger

most, is giving our people the Bible in their own language.''

''The new German Bible, which has just appeared entire,'' said Jonas, ''is a wonderful work, dear friend. How quickly it is being followed by others, in all the countries to which the Reformation has spread, put into the daily speech of the people! This is a great gift to the world.''

''Amen!'' said Dr. Martin. ''I hope that soon the workman at his bench and the housewife in her kitchen shall know more of God's Word than monks and priests did in days gone by.''

''By the way,'' said Philip, laughing, with a glance at Katherine, who had returned to the room some moments before, ''how does your 'gracious lady doctoress,' as you call Mistress Katie, get on with her task?''

''Very well, indeed,'' laughed Dr. Martin, in reply. ''She will surely earn the fifty silver florins I promised her, if she would read the new Bible through before Easter.

''My Katie is a learned woman, you must

know; only she is so busy with her farm, her house, and her children, and with the care of her troublesome husband, that she seldom takes time to read anything. But this she must read, whether she will or no!"

Katie laughed with them, as the men arose and prepared to go.

"A happy Christmas to you all!" said Jonas.

"And blessings on your roof, and all beneath it!" added Philip earnestly.

"In the name of the Christ-child!" finished Dr. Martin, as he lighted them to the door.

IN DR. MARTIN'S GARDEN

XVII

IN DR. MARTIN'S GARDEN

ON a bright summer evening Dr. Nicholas Amsdorf was strolling leisurely along toward the old monastery where his friend, Dr. Luther, made his home.

As he reached the gate leading into the garden he heard a sound unusual in that happy place; it was the sound of a child's voice crying bitterly.

He pushed open the gate and went inside.

On the grass sat little Magdalene; and in her hand lay a dead sparrow. Over her stood Hans, with boyish dislike of tears, trying to check her weeping.

"Come, sister," Nicholas heard him say, "don't cry any more; it won't make the little bird come back to life! Let's make a nice little grave and bury it!"

But Magdalene only sobbed harder.

"Listen, Lena, here is Dr. Nicholas; you don't want him to see you cry like this. Be a good girl, now!"

No use! the tears ran all the faster.

Then the voice the little girl loved best of all spoke to her gently, as Dr. Martin came down the walk.

"Dear Lena," said her father, taking the child in his arms, "it was God's little bird, you know; and God has taken it back again."

"Will it fly around and sing again, up in heaven?" asked Lena, through her tears.

"Who knows?" said her father, soothingly. "There are all sorts of beautiful things in heaven, and there must surely be little birds."

"And dogs, father!" put in Hans, around whose feet a pet puppy was tumbling. "Will there be little dogs like Clownie in heaven?"

"Why not?" said Dr. Martin, leaning down to pat the bright-eyed little animal. "In the new heavens and earth, why should there not be little dogs, with skin like silk and hair of gold, running about and playing?"

Magdalene was comforted now, and her sobbing grew quieter.

"Pardon, dear Nicholas," said Dr. Martin. "Now we can talk! Come and sit here on the bench with us, and enjoy this beautiful evening."

"Father," said Hans, earnestly. "Wolf did not trap this bird; we found it lying on the grass. Wolf has not tried to catch any birds since you read him your letter from them!"

"What is this?" asked Amsdorf, entering into the spirit of the occasion. "Have the birds been writing letters to Dr. Martin?"

"Old Wolf Sieberger, our man-of-all-work about the place," said Dr. Martin, smiling, "had set snares for the birds in the garden here. So I wrote a letter of protest, and read it to him, as if it had been sent me by the birds themselves."

"You should have seen Wolf's face!" put in Hans. "He didn't know what to say,

197

but he went out and put away all the traps. Father, let me get the letter for Dr. Nicholas to read!"

Hans was back in a twinkling, bearing a sheet of paper.

"Just listen, Dr. Nicholas!" he cried, and began to read.

"To the gracious master, Martin Luther, preacher at Wittenberg:

"We, thrushes, blackbirds, linnets, goldfinches, together with other good and honorable birds who are to journey this autumn over Wittenberg, beg to advise you that we have information that Wolf Sieberger, your servant, has paid a high price for some old, worn-out nets, that he may rig up a snare to take from us the liberty given us by God to fly in the air and gather grains of corn on the ground.

"Since this is very hard for us poor birds who have no barns nor houses, we humbly beg you to ask him to give up his plans until we have made our journey over Wittenberg.

"If he will not do this, we hope that he may be repaid by finding in his trap when morning comes, frogs, locusts, and snails instead of us!"

"That reminds me," said Nicholas, "of the letter I heard about, which your father wrote from Coburg to some of the young men who lived at that time here in the house. Have you seen that, Hans, my boy?"

"Yes," said Hans eagerly, "my mother keeps a copy of it, with the letter he wrote to me from Coburg. Shall I get them for you?"

"Hans, you will tire Dr. Nicholas with your chatter," said his father, looking up from the little grave he was digging for the dead sparrow. But Hans had already disappeared.

"Let the boy go, Martin," laughed Nicholas. "He enjoys it, and so do I. I am never happier than here among your children."

"Here it is," said Hans, coming back, breathless.

"There is a grove just under our window, like a small forest. There the jackdaws and crows are holding a diet. They fly in and out, and keep up a racket day and night without ceasing.

"I have not yet seen their emperor, but their nobles and knights constantly flit and gad about, not clothed expensively, but all in one color, all alike black and all alike gray-eyed. They sing the same song, but the voices of young and old, great and small, are different.

"They care nothing for grand palaces and halls, for their hall is vaulted with the beautiful, broad sky, its floor is paved with lovely green branches, and its walls are as wide as the world. They do not ask for horses or armor, having winged chariots on which to escape the hunter.

"They are high and mighty lords, but I don't know yet what they are deciding. So far as I can learn, they plan a great war against wheat, barley, oats, malt, and all sorts of grain; and many a one will show himself a hero, and do valiant deeds. It gives a special delight to see in how knightly a fashion they strut about, polish their bills, and prepare for victory over the grain."

"And this," said Hans, proudly unfolding another paper, "is my own letter, the first I ever got! Of course," he added, with an air of dignity, "I was just a very little boy then!"

And once more he began:

"To my dear son, Hans Luther. Grace and peace in Christ, my darling little son. I am very glad to hear that you are studying well and praying diligently. Go on doing so, my little son, and when I come home I will bring you a beautiful present.

"I know a lovely garden, where there are many children. They wear golden coats, and pick up fine apples, pears, cherries, and plums under the trees. They sing and jump and are very merry. They also have beautiful little horses, with bridles of gold and saddles of silver.

"I asked the man who owned the garden who the children were. He answered,

" 'These are the children who gladly pray and study and are good.'

"Then I said,

" 'Dear man, I also have a son, named Hans Luther. Wouldn't he like to come into the garden, and eat such beautiful apples and pears, and ride such fine horses, and play with these children?'

"Then the man said,

" 'If he prays and studies gladly and is good he, too, shall come into the garden, and his friends Lippus and Jost with him. And when they are all here, they shall have whistles and drums and lutes and all sorts of things to make music with, and they shall dance and shoot with little crossbows.'

"And he showed me a beautiful meadow in the garden, fixed for dancing. Gold whistles were hung there, and drums and silver cross-

202

bows. But it was still early, and the children had not yet eaten, so I couldn't wait for the dance, and I said to the man:

" 'Dear sir, I will go as fast as I can, and write it all to my dear son Hans, that he may study and pray well and be good, and so come into this garden. But he has an Aunt Lena whom he will have to bring with him.'

"Then the man said,

" 'Very well, go and write it to him.'

"Therefore, dear little son Hans, study and pray bravely, and tell Lippus and Jost to do so, too, and you shall all come into the garden. The dear God take care of you! Greet Auntie Lena and give her a kiss for me.

"Your loving father,

MARTIN LUTHER."

"Now, Hans," put in his father, "the letters are finished, the little bird is buried, and the dew will soon be falling. Take your little sister and go in; Dr. Nicholas and I

203

will come presently, and then we shall sing, for it is almost your bedtime."

"It is wonderful to me, Martin," said Nicholas, as the children disappeared, "how you can always take the time to play with your little ones, and write to them, when you are busy with such constant writing, lecturing, and preaching, and often when your own heart must be anxious and troubled."

"The birds have been my preachers, dear Nicholas," said Dr. Martin, pointing to a low bough in the shrubbery, where a bird sat quietly on her nest, almost within reach of their hands.

"See the little bird!" he continued. "She puts her head under her wing and goes to sleep secure in the care of the heavenly Father. So ought we to be.

"There is only one thing, dear friend, that makes us happy and peaceful and free from care. It is the promise of God. And when we read his Word and ask him to take care of us, we can all be happy together,

THE WARTBURG

A CORNER IN THE WARTBURG

LUTHER'S ROOM

though the ban of the empire hangs over us and our fears and anxieties are many. Come, let us go in and sing together,

'A mighty fortress is our God!' ''

THE LAST VICTORY

XVIII

THE LAST VICTORY

"MOTHER, mother!" cried Paul Luther, running into the living-room in high excitement, "just think! Father is going to Mansfeld next week, and he says that Hans and Martin and I may go along and visit the cousins there and in Eisenach!"

The bitter winter of 1546 had laid its cold hand on Wittenberg. Great storms had swelled the Elbe to a torrent and blocks of ice floated in the tossing waters.

The old, rambling monastery building was cold and full of unexpected drafts; but in the living-room the fire crackled cheerily.

Ten years had brought many changes to the little group around Dr. Martin's fireside. Hans, who followed Paul less eagerly into the room, was a well-grown young man of

209

almost twenty. As if to fulfil the dream of the grandfather for whom he was named, he was beginning the study of law.

Martin, the younger, who sat reading by the fire, was of lighter frame than his sturdy brothers. At fifteen, he was long and lank, with a look of frailty that often caused anxiety to the heart of Mother Katie.

Margaret, a pretty, lively girl of eleven, was sewing by her mother's side.

Sweet Magdalene had, in her fourteenth year, left the happy circle and gone to be with the Father in heaven.

Dr. Martin, coming in with slower steps behind his sons, was altered no less than they. Ceaseless toil and ill health had set their mark upon him. He walked heavily, and Katie's eyes clouded as she saw how he labored in breathing after his short walk; but his eyes were bright as ever and his greeting as cheery.

"Come into my study, dear Katie," he said to her, drawing her away from the excited little group around the fire.

"Dear husband!" exclaimed Katherine, "surely you are not going again to Mansfeld in this dreadful weather!"

"I must, Katie," said Dr. Martin gravely. "The Counts of Mansfeld have promised that they will try to come to an agreement if I will act as peacemaker between them. I have no choice but to go."

"You have already tried twice, and were away from home over Christmas on that account," said Katie, "but it failed."

"That was because Philip was taken sick and I had to bring him home again," said her husband.

"The Counts have been quarreling a long time," persisted Katie, rebelliously. "They might just as well wait till spring, and not drag you away from home again in the middle of winter, when you have been so much troubled with illness."

"Their hearts are willing now, Katie," said Dr. Martin. "If I wait, they may harden again, and I can do nothing with them."

"It is such a foolish thing to quarrel about, anyway!" said his wife, still unconvinced. "It is something so unimportant that hardly anybody seems to know what it is all about. Your health is surely worth more than the petty disputes of Count Gebhard and Count Albert."

"The cause of the quarrel, indeed, is trifling," said Dr. Martin, thoughtfully, "but the consequences are great.

"Look, dear Katie! I have taken a great task on myself. I have separated a vast body of people from the Church of Rome, and have set up a new Church which is yet feeble. I have proclaimed that there is power in God's Word and in his Spirit, to help men live right, without priests and confessors. Nobles and people have believed my word, and have staked their faith upon it. The new Church stands in the eyes of all men as a witness to the gospel.

"Now the brother Counts of my own Mansfeld are at strife. The people see the bad example. Our enemies say:

212

" 'This is a sample of your new freedom! They might have taken their quarrel to the pope, and he would have settled it, and set them both a penance to perform, and that would have been the end of it. But now there is no reverence for the Holy Father, and men do whatever they please!'

"Besides, the people suffer when their princes are at war. Often since this trouble began I have had to present to the Counts the complaints of their people, who are oppressed.

"For my own sake also, dear Katie, I cannot refuse. When the Peasants' War arose, I stood against it; I rebuked the people for rebelling against their rulers; I denounced their strife and violence. Must I not preach the same doctrine to the princes and nobles if they forget to keep the peace?"

Katie, still unreconciled, shook her head sadly, but she said no more. Silently she spent the last few days in preparing comforts for the winter journey.

Across the storm-swept country the little

company journeyed with much difficulty and many halts. At Halle, they found their way blocked for five days by the Saale river, which had flooded the land with water and broken ice.

To the worried Katie, Dr. Martin wrote back, while they waited,

"Read your Bible, dear Katie, and remember that God is almighty and could create ten Dr. Martins if the old one were drowned in the Saale. Dismiss your cares, for I have One who cares for me better than you or angels can."

Letters of anxious tone continued, however, to come from Wittenberg. Had he kept his warm coat on? Was he guarding against getting his feet wet? Would he remember—and so forth, and so forth. Katie was sure he was taking all sorts of needless risks, removed from her watchful eyes.

"Most holy Lady Doctoress!" wrote Dr. Martin at last, endeavoring to laugh away her fears. "I thank you kindly for the great anxiety which keeps you awake. Since you

214

began to worry, we have almost had a fire
in the inn just in front of my door; and yesterday, due to your anxiety no doubt, a stone
nearly fell on my head, and might have
squeezed it up as a trap does a mouse, for
in my bedroom lime and cement had dribbled
down on my head for two days, until I called
attention to it, and then the people of the
inn just touched a stone as big as a bolster
and two spans wide, which thereupon fell out
of the ceiling! For this I thank your anxiety, but the dear angels protected me. I
fear that unless you stop worrying the earth
will swallow me up!"

Meanwhile the work of reconciling the
brother Counts proceeded but slowly in the
town of Eisleben, which the travelers had at
last managed to reach.

"The lawyers make it worse with their
endless quibbling," Dr. Martin declared. "I
would gladly leave and go home, but my
duty holds me."

Finally on St. Valentine's Day, he wrote
to Katie:

"We hope to come home this week, for the Counts have settled almost everything, with the exception of two or three points, among them, that the two brothers, Count Gebhard and Count Albert, shall again be brotherly. To-day I am to undertake this, inviting them to dine with me, that they may talk together, for hitherto they have had nothing to say to each other and have written very bitterly in their letters.

"The young lords and ladies, on the other hand, are merry, go sleigh-riding together, and play masquerading.

"I am sending you the trout given me by Countess Albert. She rejoices with all her heart over the reconciliation."

Two days later, the final agreement between the Counts was completed, and signed by Martin Luther as a witness. The victory was won; the brothers had met as friends once more.

"Now we can go home!" he exclaimed exultingly to Dr. Jonas, when at last the weary business was at an end.

But the exposures and hardships of the journey had been too much for the weakened frame.

Early on the morning of the eighteenth of February his friends and his three sons were called in haste, to speed the tired warrior on his homeward way.

"The faith, dear father, which you have taught," said they, "is it yours to the end?"

Clearly and firmly rang out the answer, "Yes!"

Then the victor passed on to his triumph.

"He died for us!" said the reconciled Counts, standing by the quiet bedside.

Nay, not for you alone, brother Counts of Mansfeld, but for the mighty cause of peace on earth, since all men are brothers.

THE TORCH-BEARERS

THE TORCH-BEARERS

IN days of old, when great news came of
mighty happenings by land or sea, fleet
runners were chosen and equipped with
flaming torches to bear the word abroad.

Up to the beacon on the nearest hilltop
ran the first, and kindled there the flame that
told of victory. Then another distant waiting athlete saw the flaring signal and
hastened to set the next beacon-fire blazing
on its hilltop.

On and on went the fiery message till all
the land was lit with the good news and every
city and hamlet rejoiced.

So, after the Dark Ages there came a man
who kindled the beacon of a new day; and
the flaming torch he bore was the Book of

God, given to the people in words that they could understand.

Land after land all over the continent of Europe caught fire. Everywhere the Bible was translated into the language of the people; and still the light sped on.

Then God opened the doors of the New World by the hand of explorers and discoverers; and wherever the Western Continent was peopled by men and women from the lands of the Reformation, there may be found the open Bible and liberty of conscience.

Once more God pointed the way, and men went forth to rediscover the ancient East. And everywhere, in the footprints of the traveler, has gone the man with the kindled torch.

Carey in India, Moffat in Africa, Morrison in China, Judson in Burma—the work of each has been the same. Under foreign skies, through heat and thirst and fever, threatened by enemies, persecuted and imprisoned, they have toiled with the same great purpose that

inspired the lonely outlaw in the Wartburg
—to spread far and wide the Word of God,
in the simple, daily language of the people.

And still the flaming line flashes on. But
the hand that lifted the light high and sent it
kindling on its way was the hand, in God's
good providence, of Martin Luther.